My
Italian Wedding

by Anthony J. Wilkinson

A SAMUEL FRENCH ACTING EDITION

SAMUEL FRENCH

FOUNDED 1830

NEW YORK HOLLYWOOD LONDON TORONTO

SAMUELFRENCH.COM

ISBN 978-0-573-69927-6   Printed in U.S.A.   #29766

MUSIC USE NOTE

Licensees are solely responsible for obtaining formal written permission from copyright owners to use copyrighted music in the performance of this play and are strongly cautioned to do so. If no such permission is obtained by the licensee, then the licensee must use only original music that the licensee owns and controls. Licensees are solely responsible and liable for all music clearances and shall indemnify the copyright owners of the play and their licensing agent, Samuel French, Inc., against any costs, expenses, losses and liabilities arising from the use of music by licensees.

If licensees If the producing company wishes to include the music from the original production, they can obtain **performance and rehearsal CDs** by the The Susan Gurman Agency, LLC, 245 West 99th Street, New York, New York 10025.

IMPORTANT BILLING AND CREDIT
REQUIREMENTS

All producers of *MY BIG GAY ITALIAN WEDDING must* give credit to the Author of the Play in all programs distributed in connection with performances of the Play, and in all instances in which the title of the Play appears for the purposes of advertising, publicizing or otherwise exploiting the Play and/or a production. The name of the Author *must* appear on a separate line on which no other name appears, immediately following the title and *must* appear in size of type not less than fifty percent of the size of the title type.

PRODUCTION HISTORY

My Big Gay Italian Wedding premiered Off Broadway at the Actor's Play-house in November, 2003 where it played in repertory with the musical *Naked Boys Singing*. It was directed by Peter Rapanaro and starred Anthony J. Wilkinson and Bill Fischer. The show also featured costume design by Chris March of Bravo's reality television series *Project Runway*. After six months of over sold houses, the production moved to a larger venue (Theatre Four) where it continued its run till the end of 2004.

On September 12, 2009, a revised and updated version of the script, played a benefit performance at the St. George Theatre in Staten Island. The new production was produced by Dina Manzo and Sonia Blangiardo. The show starred its creator Anthony J. Wilkinson as well as Scott Evans of the ABC soap opera *One Life to Live*. It was directed and also produced by Teresa A. Cicala and included new choreography by J. Austin Eyer.

The revised production moved to an open-ended Equity run at the St. Luke's Theatre Off Broadway in May 2010, adding original music by David Boyd and Reichen Lehmkuhl of CBS TV's *The Amazing Race*, as Wilkinson's co-star.

On August 2, 2010, it was announced that *Real Housewives of New Jersey* cast members Teresa Giudice, Caroline Manzo, Lauren Manzo, Jacqueline Laurita and Ashley Holmes would step in as cast members for one week in September. After sold-out performances, the Housewives signed up to repeat their guest appearances on October 20th to 23rd.

As of January, 2011, the show continues to run successfully Off-Broadway at St. Luke's Theatre.

A NOTE ON THE MUSIC

The original production of *My Big Gay Italian Wedding* contained 4 original songs by David James Boyd. While the lyrics of these songs are still printed in this script, licensees are welcome to select music of their own choosing in place of the music performed in the play.

Please note that licensees are solely responsible for obtaining formal written permission from copyright owners to use copyrighted music in the performance of this play and are strongly cautioned to do so. If no such permission is obtained by the licensee, then the licensee must use only original music that the licensee owns and controls. Licensees are solely responsible and liable for all music clearances and shall indemnify the copyright owners of the play and their licensing agent, Samuel French, Inc., against any costs, expenses, losses and liabilities arising from the use of music by licensees.

If the producing company wishes to include the music from the original production, they can obtain **performance and rehearsal CDs** by the The Susan Gurman Agency, LLC, 245 West 99th Street, New York, New York 10025.

CHARACTERS

ANTHONY PINNUNZIATO – 20s-30s male. Our every-man. Pollyanna guido from Bay Ridge. LEAD

ANDREW POLINSKI – late 20s-30s male. Handsome and stylish, yet devoted to one man only. Dashing and charming. LEAD

ANGELA PINNUNZIATO – late 40s female. A lovingly over-bearing, over-powering Italian mother hen. Rules the roost with an irori fist and a wooden spatula. Anthony's mother. LEAD.

JOSEPH PINNUNZIATO/FATHER ROSALIA – late 40s male. Joseph is Anthony's loud Italian father whose word is law and whose home is his castle. Father Rosalia is the crush of every parishioner, both male and female. Tries hard to resist the temptations of flesh, both male and female. Note: These two roles can be played by the same actor if needed. LEAD

MAURIZIO LEGRANDE – late 20s-40s male. Outlandishly dressed, over the top, flamboyant wedding coordinator. Has an accent that cannot be pegged down. LEAD

GREGORIO – 20s -30s male. Smoking hot and extremely narcissistic. Does not take rejection well. Always has something up his sleeve. LEAD.

MARIO – 20s-30s male. Uptight fashionista, Anthony's best friend and protector. The most fabulous dancer in Brooklyn. Anthony's Best Man. SUPPORTING.

LUCIA – 20s - 30s female. Brassy, trendy Italian woman. Anthony's dependable, reliable best friend. A feminine, pretty lipstick lesbian, classy and sophisticated until challenged. Maid of Honor. SUPPORTING.

CONNIE – 20s - 30s female. Lucia's nemesis. Just as pretty, but much tougher. The gum chewing mouth of a truck driver who doesn't take crap from anyone. Bridesmaid. SUPPORTING.

MARIA – 20s female. Anthony's flighty, heavy-set, sweet and self-absorbed baby sister. Aspirations of stardom, but a fizzled sense of reality. She is a Broadway actress wannabe and fancies herself a tremendous singer. SUPPORTING

RODNEY – 30s male. Sassy and spirited. Always up for an adventure. In love with Frankie. Reveals himself in drag in Act Two. All ethnicities can work in this role.

AUNT TONIANN – 30s-early 40s female. Angela's fussy younger Italian sister. Lives to torment her brother-in-law. Sports the biggest of hair and always (thinks she's) dressed to the nines. SUPPORTING

FRANKIE – late 20s-late 30s male. Tough, good-looking Italian stud. No-nonsense, out, and proud. The straight acting gay guy in the bunch. Groomsman. SUPPORTING

ACKNOWLEDGEMENTS

With the support of special friends and family, visions like this can become a reality.

Special thanks to Sonia Blangiardo and Teresa Anne Cicala for their continued efforts and hard work on this project, for without them it would not exist.

I dedicate this show to my best friend and mother whose love and devotion continues to make me stronger. To my late father, who set the bar for what a true man really is. Thank you God for giving me parents who never judged, allowed me to be creative and speak my voice, and most of all... taught me to love myself.

– *Anthony J. Wilkinson*

PROLOGUE

(Onstage, four traditional heterosexual couples dance a traditional version of the "Tarantella." Mid-way through the dance, a techno version of that song crashes in, and two of the couples change partners and begin to dance not so traditionally…one of the original couples is not able to adapt to the new style and runs off, while the other decide all is well and allow themselves to let loose and dance along with the non-traditional couples as a new harmonious age is born.)

ACT 1

Scene I:
The Pinnunziato House

(We begin in a typical Brooklyn-Italian kitchen. **ANGELA PINNUNZIATO** *[a lovingly overbearing, overpowering, Italian mother hen who rules the roost with an iron fist and a wooden spatula] and her husband* **JOSEPH PINNUNZIATO** *[balding, slightly paunchy, loud Italian whose word is law and whose home is his castle] are onstage.* **ANGELA** *is starting to cook dinner and is growing more and more frustrated that no one is helping her.* **JOSEPH** *is watching TV.)*

JOSEPH. Oh shit! Double-play!

ANGELA. Joseph, can you help me peel the potatoes?

JOSEPH. Holy crap! He missed the base. Oh, thank God he's safe.

ANGELA. Joseph!! Can you help me peel the potatoes?

JOSEPH. I'm watching the game!

ANGELA. I know! God forbid you get off your fat ass and help me do something for a change!

JOSEPH. Get one of the kids to help you!!

ANGELA. That'll be the day. I never get any help in this house. I do everything and everyone just sits around and expects it all to get done. You know what? One day I'm gonna drop dead and no one will know what to do.

JOSEPH. I know, then who's gonna make the meatballs as lousy as you do!

ANGELA. Sure Joseph, joke around and sit nice while I run around crazy as usual. And then we wonder why all the doctors tell me I have an ulcer, I have colitis. It's my nerves!

JOSEPH. It's menopause honey, it ain't your nerves!

ANGELA. What would you know about menopause, Joey!??

(ANTHONY PINNUNZIATO [cute and funny Italian-American man who is somewhat naïve to the real world] enters from work.)

ANTHONY. Oh Madonna! I heard you two screaming on eighteenth avenue! What is the problem!?

ANGELA. I asked your father to do me one simple favor and peel the potatoes and God forbid he gets up!

ANTHONY. Ma! I'll do it, gimme.

ANGELA. Oh finally, someone helps me. See Joseph, your son is gonna help me!

JOSEPH. He wants something!

ANTHONY. I don't want anything, Dad.

JOSEPH. We'll see.

ANGELA. Thank you, Anthony! Mommy can always use a hand in the kitchen. At least somebody appreciates me!

(MARIA PINNUNZIATO [Anthony's flighty, sweet, and self-absorbed baby sister, who has aspirations of stardom and, like her brother, a somewhat fizzled sense of reality,] enters.)

MARIA. Ma!

ANGELA. What?

MARIA. Ma!

ANGELA. What?

MARIA. MA!

ANGELA. WHAT?!?

MARIA. Tomorrow me and Claudia are going into the city for the open audition of *Mamma Mia*, here I go again, my my, I cannot resist ya!

ANGELA. That's wonderful, honey.

MARIA. I'm gonna be a Broadway star!

ANGELA. Joseph, did you hear that…your daughter is gonna be a Broadway star!

JOSEPH. Of course she is! She gets that beautiful voice of hers from my side of the family.

ANGELA. Broadway star, make the salad.

MARIA. What, no smart remarks, Anthony?

ANTHONY. I think it's a beautiful thing, Maria.

MARIA. WHAT!? You mean you're not gonna tell me I suck? What the Hell is wrong with you today?

ANTHONY. Nothing is wrong with me. It's just that something wonderful happened to me last night.

MARIA. Oooh! What happened?

(**ANTHONY** *holds up his ring finger to show the engagement ring.*)

MARIA. Ma!

ANGELA. What?

MARIA. Ma!

ANGELA. What?

MARIA. MA!

ANGELA. WHAT?!?

MARIA. Look!

(**ANGELA** *turns her head and sees* **ANTHONY** *holding up his hand.*)

ANGELA. What's the matter, you cut yourself, honey?

MARIA. Ma, he's engaged!

ANGELA. Engaged!!!

ANTHONY. Andrew and I are getting married.

ANGELA. Over my dead body you're getting married.

ANTHONY. Mom!!

ANGELA. JOSEPH!!! Get over here, I'm gonna have heart failure, your son is trying to kill me!!!

JOSEPH. What's the matter??

ANGELA. Your son wants to get married! Maria, get me a chair before I pass out.

(**MARIA** *gets her a chair.*)

JOSEPH. I told you he wanted something.

ANGELA. I'm having a panic attack.

JOSEPH. Angela calm down...

ANTHONY. Ma, you're overreacting...as usual! You know that I have been seeing Andrew for a year now. What's the big deal?

ANGELA. The big deal!!! You're gay! You think it's normal for two men to parade around town getting married!

MARIA. Oh Anthony, this is so exciting, how did this happen? Did you propose like straight people do?

ANTHONY. Well...here's what happened. Last night, Andrew and I went out with some friends to that new karaoke bar in the village. And it was such a beautiful night, we decided to walk back to his place.

(*The stage goes dark and a spotlight shines on* **ANTHONY** *and* **ANDREW POLINSKI** *[handsome and stylish, he looks like a "player" but swears his devotion is to one man only] as he enters and they re-enact the night before.*)

ANDREW. Ready to go baby?

ANTHONY. I can't believe you just left me hanging there on stage for OUR duet. Doing Barbra Streisand is hard enough, but Donna too?!

ANDREW. You know I don't sing. Never have. Never will.

ANTHONY. Not even for me?

ANDREW. Not even for you.

(**ANDREW** *pulls pouting* **ANTHONY** *to him.*)

I still love you though.

ANTHONY. I love you, too.

ANDREW. Yeah?

ANTHONY. Yeah.

(They kiss, it gets a little heated, and **ANDREW** *pulls away.)*

ANDREW. Screw walking. Let's get a taxi.

ANTHONY. Andrew, wait....I actually want to talk to you about something. And this is the perfect time and place to do it.

ANDREW. Okay...?

ANTHONY. Andrew, what would you say if I suggested you and I get married?

ANDREW. Married? Like, *married* married? How much have you had to drink?

ANTHONY. No, I'm serious.

ANDREW. How serious?

*(***ANTHONY*** kneels down and proposes, first pulling out a cloth to put down on the floor so his pants don't get dirty. Once he kneels, he reaches into his pocket and pulls out a beautiful engagement ring.)*

ANTHONY. Marry me, Andrew Polinski.

ANDREW. Oh shit.

*(***ANTHONY*** jumps up.)*

ANTHONY. Forget it. I can't believe I did this. Just forget this ever happened. I never asked this question –

ANDREW. No! No, wait. It's just that I never thought about marriage. It's not something I ever pictured, or even thought was possible.

ANTHONY. I know. Let's just say I was drunk and pretend this never happened.

ANDREW. No. I don't want to do that. I never pictured myself getting married, but now I'm picturing it. With you. I know I want to be with you. And I know that feeling will never change. So let's do it. Let's get hitched!

(They kiss, then **ANTHONY** *holds up the ring again.* **ANDREW** *offers his hand and* **ANTHONY** *puts the ring on him. They kiss again, then* **ANDREW** *pulls away.)*

ANDREW. Wait. What about your ring?

ANTHONY. I don't need a ring.

ANDREW. Yes, you do. Here.

(**ANDREW** *pulls off one of his own rings and kneels.*)

ANTHONY. But that was your father's ring!

ANDREW. I know. I want you to have it.

(**ANDREW** *kneels, then places the ring on* **ANTHONY**'*s finger, and they embrace.* **ANDREW** *throws his arm over* **ANTHONY**'*s shoulder and they start to stroll off.*)

ANTHONY. So I'm thinking a big hall, with no more than 300 people –

(**ANDREW** *exits but* **ANGELA** *grabs* **ANTHONY**'*s arm and pulls him back to reality.*)

ANGELA. Anthony, I love you dearly. But there is no way I am going to allow you to get married. I mean what kind of wedding were you thinking of having?

ANTHONY. A big traditional wedding, with the whole family in a big hall –

ANGELA. Have you lost your mind? Joseph, talk to him please, before I have a stroke.

JOSEPH. *Mama Mia!* First Obama and now this? And who the Hell is gonna pay for this wedding?

ANTHONY. Daddy…

JOSEPH. Don't "Daddy" me on this one!

ANTHONY. I knew you two were gonna act this way! You never accepted the fact that I'm gay!

ANGELA. How dare you say that!!! Have I not been nothing but nice to all your boyfriends for the last five years?! Have I not let all your crazy friends into my house and welcomed them and fed them? Have your father and I not given you everything you could possibly want since the day you were born?! Anthony Giuseppe Pinnunziato how could you want to embarrass me like this?

ANTHONY. Because I'm in love, Mom. And the same way you fell in love with Daddy and wanted to share that love with the rest of the important people in your life…that's how I feel. And it shouldn't make a difference if I'm gay or straight; and if me falling in love and getting married embarrasses you, then you don't give a damn about me!

JOSEPH. Watch your mouth!

ANTHONY. No, Dad…I'm sorry that I am upset, but for the first time ever in my life I have found my soulmate. Someone that I know I will spend the rest of my life with. And all I want is what everyone else in this family had. I want a wedding. I want to be committed in the eyes of God –

ANGELA. You should be committed all right…

ANTHONY. – and I want my parents blessing in helping me do this. Can't you give me that much?

ANGELA. How does what's-his-face's family feel about this?

ANTHONY. *Andrew* doesn't have much of a family. His father's dead and his mother lives in Florida; they don't speak.

MARIA. Oh, that's so sad. Can I sing at the wedding?

ANTHONY. Of course you can, Maria…If Mommy and Daddy let me have one.

ANGELA. Joseph…

JOSEPH. Don't look at me, you're the one with the ulcers!

ANGELA. You're the one that's gonna pay for this.

JOSEPH. Well, if we decided to do this…no son of mine is getting married in some *scoumbari* wedding hall. Bacci's for my son!

ANGELA. If we do agree to this, we have to do it the right way of course.

ANTHONY. Of course, and Mom…will you give me away?

ANGELA. Anthony, why don't you just put a freakin' gun to my head and just shoot me, it will be that much easier!

ANTHONY. Ma….

ANGELA. All right! I'll give you away at your wedding.

(**ANTHONY** *grabs his mother, truly happy.*)

ANTHONY. Okay, so I'm going to go call Bacci's, see what dates they have open.

ANGELA. Not so fast.

ANTHONY. What?

ANGELA. Before you start booking halls, there a few things we need to discuss.

ANTHONY. Okay…..

ANGELA. I want Father Rosalia to perform the service.

JOSEPH. That's a must.

ANTHONY. But Mom, he's a catholic priest!

ANGELA. And we are a Catholic family and that is how I raised you.

ANTHONY. But Andrew's family isn't even Catholic. And I don't know if we can get married in church.

ANGELA. You can have the ceremony at Bacci's but ONLY Father Rosalia can perform the service. I will not allow this unless he does. And…and I want what's-his-face's – *Andrew's* mother at the wedding. What background are they?

ANTHONY. Well, he's mostly Polish but –

(**JOSEPH** *spits out his drink and starts to choke.*)

Well, his grandmother I think is actually Irish and German!

(**JOSEPH** *continues to choke even harder.*)

Actually, I think the father's great-grandmother was Puerto Rican!

(**JOSEPH** *falls to the floor and* **MARIA** *goes over to assist.*)

JOSEPH. This is it Angela. I'm heading toward the light!

ANTHONY. I don't know why you are all worked up about what background they are because he doesn't speak to his mother anyway!

ANGELA. Well, he is going to start. Because I will not stand up there alone. I don't care where she lives. I'll fly her out here if I have to. If you don't have her blessing then I can't give mine.

(AUNT TONIANN [Angela's fussy younger sister, who lives to torment her brother-in-law] enters.)

TONIANN. Oh my God, the traffic today.... Angela, you got any coffee perkin'?

(She sees JOSEPH on the floor.)

Oh Jesus, he had a heart attack? It's probably *acida* from all that spicy food you ate last night.

ANGELA. It's not the spicy food, it's the stress. We just heard some news today.

TONIANN. Oh my God...you heard!

ANGELA. Yes, we heard! How long have you known?

TONIANN. *Aiutarmi Gesu!* I need some coffee for this.

(MARIA runs to help her aunt.)

ANTHONY. Wait, I don't understand. When did you find out? This just happened –

TONIANN. Anthony, Aunt Toniann is no fool. I've known for the last few months that Salvatore Giancarlo, the love of my life, is...a married man.

(There's a moment of stunned silence.)

JOSEPH. What!??

ANGELA. You're dating a married man? You brought a married man into this house? And let me feed him, and be nice to him? A MARRIED MAN? Toniann!

TONIANN. I was actually coming to talk to you about it., but that big mouth, Ondine Ozzupacci found out and next thing you know it's all over Brooklyn!

MARIA. Psst! That's not what they were talking about.

AUNT TONIANN. Oh? Crap.

JOSEPH. I'm so glad I lived to see the day. Little Miss Righteous over here is some *cetriolo's Conmare*! *(trans. "loser's mistress")*

AUNT TONIANN. I knew it was too good to be true that you were dead.

(**ANTHONY** *jumps in to stop the argument.*)

ANTHONY. Aunt Toniann, I'm getting married!

TONIANN. Oh Anthony! That's so nice! But I didn't know it was legal now?

ANTHONY. Well, it's really not…

TONIANN. That's because that bigot Angelina Azzupetta DiGiacomo wrote that horrible column about gay people in the *Staten Island Advance.* I wish people would just mind their own business.

ANGELA. Speaking of which, I need to finish this with my son, would you mind giving us a few minutes? And then we *will* discuss Salvatore.

TONIANN. Oh my God, of course. Anthony, Aunt Toniann supports you no matter what! Nobody should judge you or who you sleep with.

(**JOSEPH** *"coughs."*)

JOSEPH. Putana!

TONIANN. I'm gonna go next door to Cousin Josephine's, to watch the Real Housewives of New Jersey.

(**TONIANN** *leaves.*)

ANTHONY. Okay, so we're all good, right? As long as Andrew's mother comes up for the wedding –

MARIA. And your little sister sings at the ceremony.

JOSEPH. Maria sings at the wedding.

ANTHONY. Fine.

MARIA. And she's the flower girl.

JOSEPH. And she's the flower girl.

ANTHONY. Fine. Anything else?

ANGELA. No, that's it. For now, anyway. Now I gotta go lay down before I develop an aneurysm! Between you and your aunt, I'm gonna be dead before I'm fifty. Broadway Star, watch the sausage and the broccoli rabe.

(She exits.)

JOSEPH. Anthony…

ANTHONY. Yes, Daddy…

JOSEPH. Good luck, son. Let me know how much it is. Do everything the right way. Whatever you need, let me know, and Daddy will take care of it.

ANTHONY. Thank you, Daddy.

JOSEPH. I love you, son.

ANTHONY. I love you, too.

(They hug and **JOSEPH** *exits.)*

MARIA. I'm so excited, Anthony. I just love weddings. I want to help you with this…

ANTHONY. I need all the help I can get on this one.

MARIA. Okay. First things first. Let's go pick out the songs I'm going to sing.

*(***MARIA*** grabs his hand and tugs him offstage.)*

(blackout)

Scene II
Andrew's Apartment

(**ANDREW** *is wearing only a cute pair of boxer shorts and is lounging in bed, looking at his laptop.* **ANTHONY** *is offstage in the bathroom. "My Italian Girl" plays in the background.**)

ANDREW. So maybe what we can do since the whole gay marriage thing hasn't been passed in New York yet is get married somewhere in Jersey...at least they allow Civil Unions. California's got that whole Prop 8 on again off again thing...Wait...what about Maine? I think it was legal there recently. They passed it!

(*He hits a key on the computer.*)

No they un-passed it. Huh. Okay....oh, Vermont! That's perfect!

(**ANTHONY**, *in cute pj's, enters, toothbrush in hand,*)

ANTHONY. Oh My God! It's a sign!

ANDREW. What's a sign?

ANTHONY. Do you hear what song is playing?

ANDREW. Do you like it?

ANTHONY. It's "My Italian Girl." It was my grandparents' wedding song. My grandmother said that on their first date in Coney Island, my grandfather stood up on top of the sausage and pepper stand and sang this to her. She said it was at that moment she knew she would marry him!

ANDREW. Now I see why you're such a romantic. Well, I've been doing some research and I found the most romantic spot for our wedding....are you ready.... VERMONT!

ANTHONY. Vermont? After all that work I did to convince my parents to give us a wedding? Now you want me to tell them that everyone's gotta go running to Vermont?

---

* Please see "A Note About the Music" on page 4.

ANDREW. Well, just the important people. I mean anyone important won't mind traveling, right?

ANTHONY. How do you think my Aunt Carmela and my cousin Josephine are gonna manage going all the way to Vermont? They get out of breath going up the stairs!

ANDREW. They're not walking there!

ANTHONY. What wedding halls are in Vermont anyway??

ANDREW. Well, who says we need a hall? Maybe we could get married by a lake?

ANTHONY. A lake? Where? Outside?!

ANDREW. That's usually where they are.

ANTHONY. Then my cousin Teresa won't come, she hates the bugs. And what if it rains!? Or snows! It could be a disaster…I don't understand, we got Bacci's, the nicest hall in Brooklyn. Why do you want to travel to another state???

ANDREW. I just figure if it's not legal here, something doesn't feel right about it. I don't want our wedding to turn into some big spectacle.

ANTHONY. A spectacle? Have you met my family? Let me ask you a question. Do you love me?

ANDREW. Yes.

ANTHONY. Do you want to spend your life with me?

ANDREW. Yes.

ANTHONY. Then I don't understand why we gotta keep it such a big secret?

ANDREW. That's not what I'm doing!

ANTHONY. Come on Andrew, we know that public displays of affection are just not your strong suit. I mean if karaoke wasn't a perfect example –

ANDREW. I can't believe it still bothers you that I didn't get up and sing! Did you see how many people were there?

ANTHONY. Yeah, and I didn't care! Because I love you and I would shout it and sing it right in the middle of Penn Station.

ANDREW. This whole big wedding thing just makes me so nervous.

ANTHONY. Look, I know you don't come from a big family, but I do. I spent my whole life going to weddings. Aunts, Uncles, Cousins, Friends...and the whole time I sat there in awe, because I was so happy for them. I said you know one day, I want to fall in love and share all that happiness with all the important people in my life. Andrew, I know we're different, but if you love me and I love you...there is nothing more worth celebrating than that.

ANDREW. Okay, you win! You win! We'll get married right here in Brooklyn!

(They embrace.)

ANTHONY. I have an idea...

ANDREW. Me too...

ANTHONY. Maybe at the reception you and I can come shooting out from the dancefloor in a big waterfall and sing our wedding song as a duet –

ANDREW. Anthony!

ANTHONY. We could hire the gay men's chorus to sing back up –

ANDREW. ANTHONY!

ANTHONY. A fifty foot harp could play right in the middle of the dance floor, how gorgeous would that look with all the little kids running around the Cannoli table –

*(**ANDREW** covers his mouth.)*

ANDREW. Wedding, yes...singing, no.

ANTHONY. Dancing?

ANDREW. Get over here, you.

(They start kissing.)

ANTHONY. We could take lessons!

ANDREW. I'll give you a lesson...!

(ANDREW starts to take off ANTHONY's shirt then Anthony's cell phone rings. He reluctantly untangles himself and picks it up.)

ANTHONY. Hi, Ma. Yes, I'll be ready in twenty minutes, I just gotta jump in the shower...no, I'm at Andrew's... yes, I slept over...Yes, in the same bed...I'm not going there with you. I'll be ready. Bye.

(He hangs up, and crosses back to the bed where ANDREW is still sitting. ANDREW tries to pick up where they left off before the phone call as ANTHONY rambles on.)

That was my mother. I totally forgot we were going Bacci's to sample the menu. I gotta tell you, I'm all worked up about this whole potato situation. I know they like to do either the mashed or croquettes, but what if somebody's on a diet? I mean, you really should have a baked option, no?

ANDREW. If it makes you happy, do all three.

ANTHONY. Awww. Good idea.

(They kiss and just as things get heated ANTHONY pulls away.)

I can't.

ANDREW. Why not?

ANTHONY. My mother's waiting.

ANDREW. So let her wait.

ANTHONY. Ok.

(ANTHONY pulls the covers over them. The phone rings again.)

ANDREW. Don't answer that.

ANTHONY. Do you want my mother banging down the door?

ANDREW. Fine.

(ANTHONY stumbles over to the phone.)

ANTHONY. Oh, there's no traffic, you're doing ninety on the Belt Parkway? I'll be ready in ten minutes.

(**ANTHONY** *exits to the bathroom. There is a knock at the door, then before* **ANDREW** *can respond* **GREGORIO SALINARI** *[smoking hot and extremely narcissistic man who does not take rejection well], breezes in.*)

GREGORIO. Knock, knock! Hot guido alert! Oh. My. God! You are not going to believe the rumor going around Potions last night!

ANDREW. Well, it must be good if you're making house calls!

GREGORIO. Well, you never return phone calls or texts so I figure you must be SUPER BUSY! But you are going to laugh your ass off when you hear this! The rumor going around is that the reason you have been out of the loop...is YOU are getting married!

(**GREGORIO** *bursts out laughing, and slowly realizes he is laughing alone.*)

What...you don't think that's funny?

ANDREW. I...am...getting married.

GREGORIO. That's what I said! Isn't that hysterical?

ANDREW. No, I mean I really am, Gregorio...I'm getting married for real.

GREGORIO. Ewwww! Why the hell would you want to do that? Just to make a statement you go and propose to some random trick??

ANDREW. Anthony is not some random trick!

GREGORIO. Anthony? Anthony who?? Oh...MY...GOD!! *Ant'ney?!* That Pollyanna guido from Bay Ridge *Ant'ney?* You've been seeing him for all of five minutes!

ANDREW. Gregorio, we've been seeing each other for over a year.

GREGORIO. Oh please! Not on my calendar!

ANDREW. And what calendar is that??

GREGORIO. I mean it's not like we've slept together any time during the past year...Oh wait!! We totally have!!

ANDREW. Gregorio...

GREGORIO. Memorial Day Weekend...Fire Island...Ice Palace...

ANDREW. Stop...

GREGORIO. Ahhh...yes....you were taking a weekend to yourself to "evaluate your relationship" and while Anthony was off at some lesbian barbeque...you got a little wasted with *mwah* in the pines...and if I remember correctly where we wound up....

ANDREW. I was drunk...we both were. And I was confused! I wasn't sure I wanted a commitment. I can't believe you're bringing this up!

GREGORIO. I can't believe you're going to be a total hypocrite and get married!! And even worse, act like we never existed. How could you do this to me?

ANDREW. Why is everything all about you?? It's about me and Anthony now! I love him! What happened between us was a mistake from day one!

*(**GREGORIO** is stunned speechless and takes a dramatic moment to collect himself.)*

Right?

GREGORIO. Mistake....I'm sorry, Andrew, I need to take a moment to comprehend that my first boyfriend...my first lover...my first in every way possible!!...was a "mistake!!!"

ANDREW. I can't believe you are acting like this! We were together for less than a month and that was over five years ago! And now you want to hold a one-night stand over my head.

GREGORIO. You're right....so right....if Anthony can forgive you for tricking around in Fire Island with an old fling...then who the Hell am I to judge?

ANDREW. Anthony...doesn't know about what happened between us Memorial Day Weekend.

GREGORIO. Oh?

ANDREW. That's in the past...my past! He doesn't need to know all that right?

GREGORIO. Of course not! Come on! You know me…I don't go around making house calls to spread "rumors." What happens in Fire Island…stays in Fire Island.

ANDREW. Thank You.

GREGORIO. Now, tell me about the wedding. When? Where? Are we running off to Iowa or what?

(ANDREW tries herding him towards the door.)

ANDREW. No we are actually having something right here in Brooklyn…

(ANDREW starts to show him out.)

Listen, I actually have so much to do…I was right in the middle of….

GREGORIO. Will I be invited?

ANDREW. Invited? Uh…well I think we we're gonna keep it small….

GREGORIO. Oh my God….I'm like your closest friend! How small could the guest list be?

ANDREW. I'm not sure yet….I'll totally keep you posted….

GREGORIO. Andrew….don't shut me out. Seriously, if our friendship means anything, just include me.

ANDREW. I'm not sure I know how, Gregorio.

GREGORIO. You'll find a way! You're a man of your word… right? Call me!!

(GREGORIO leaves. ANDREW is stunned speechless and drops down to the bed. A spotlight comes up on GREGORIO, who pulls out his cell phone and makes a call.)

GREGORIO. Fabrizio, it's Gregorio Salinari…I'm fabulous! Darling, I'm gonna need a tux.

(blackout)

Scene III
Rodney's Apartment

(We open in Rodney's apartment as **RODNEY JONES** *** *[a sassy and spirited man who is in love with Frankie and is always up for an adventure], plays hostess. Already present are* **CONNIE SCUCCIFUFFIO** *[a striking but tough lesbian who doesn't take crap from anyone],* **FRANKIE FALCONE** *[a tough, good-looking stud with heavy Brooklyn accent and a no-nonsense, 'I'm gay and if you don't like it go fuck yourself' attitude] and* **MARIO NICASTRO** *[an uptight, flamboyant, fashionista gay man with a napoleonic complex, who fancies himself as Anthony's best friend and protector].)*

FRANKIE. Does anyone even know what we're doing here?

RODNEY. All I know is Maria said it was important. Apparently not important enough to be on time, but whatever.

*(***LUCIA FUCCIO** *[the feminine lesbian who is also Anthony's responsible, dependable best friend], enters.)*

LUCIA. I know why we're here.

CONNIE. What the Hell is she doing here?

LUCIA. I was invited, what the Hell are you doing here?

CONNIE. Sit on the other side.

LUCIA. Back off, Connie!

CONNIE. Bad hair day?

LUCIA. It's called modern and trendy.

CONNIE. It's called dated and tacky.

LUCIA. Do you even own a mirror? Because Marcia Brady called, she wants her jeans back.

CONNIE. Jealous Jan? You always were. And FYI, you look like a cheap white trash *puttana!*

LUCIA. Well, at least I'm getting offers.

CONNIE. From who, Jenny Craig?

---

* * *If Rodney is African American, please see Addendum C*

(LUCIA and CONNIE charge at each other. FRANKIE jumps up and gets in between them.)

FRANKIE. *Aspette!* You two need to get over it. Could someone enlighten me on this?

RODNEY. You don't want to know.

LUCIA. I'll tell you what happened Frankie…Connie left me for Gianna Sclafani, my ex.

RODNEY. Oooh, she's a slut.

CONNIE. Like you were so perfect.

RODNEY. Here we go again.

LUCIA. Of all people to leave me for, you leave me for the one person on this earth I hate the most, Gianna Sclafani.

MARIO. It never ends, believe me…this happened four years ago and they're still talking about it!

RODNEY. Oh, you don't have to tell me! This comes up on my tweets every other hour!

MARIO. And now no one is with Gianna, Gianna is with that crazy blonde from Flatbush, what's her name?

FRANKIE. Tina Lantini?

RODNEY. Uh huh. Now you should read her tweets!

CONNIE. Don't even get me started on that bitch!

LUCIA. Oh, you didn't feel that way when you two were an item back in the day now, did you!?

MARIO. Lucia…

LUCIA. Then Tina turned around and left you for Rosemary Carpuccio!

RODNEY. She's a big slut.

MARIO. Oh Jesus, who could keep up with these lesbians.

FRANKIE. I thought the guys were bad.

(MARIA enters.)

CONNIE. You were jealous of all my past girlfriends from day one and you still are.

LUCIA. Jealous of Tina Lantini? Oh, yes! My envy runs deep! That skank makes those Jersey Shore girls look like saints. I'm so glad to hear you raised your standards.

CONNIE. Go to Hell, Lucia!

(CONNIE lunges at LUCIA, and FRANKIE intercepts her.)

FRANKIE. Yo, straight guys get off on this.

MARIO. Seriously?

CONNIE. You're lucky he's holding me back.

MARIA. Ladies!! Ladies!! Please! This is a party for my brother. Can everyone at least try to get along?!

CONNIE. This better be important because it stinks around here.

LUCIA. Yeah, it does.

MARIO. What is this about anyway, Maria?

FRANKIE. Yeah it's disco night at Paradise.

(ANTHONY enters.)

ANTHONY. Disco night can wait, Frankie.

(All ad-lib greetings.)

FRANKIE. But, I got a hot date with Danny Teneglia.

ANTHONY. Danny Teneglia can wait, too. I have a very special announcement I would like to make to my closest and dearest friends.

MARIO. You dumped Andrew?

ANTHONY. No Mario, we're getting married.

(He shows everyone the ring. Everyone is stunned in a cheerful way except MARIO who is huffy and annoyed. FRANKIE whistles.)

FRANKIE. Break out the Cold Duck!

RODNEY. Quack, quack, baby!

LUCIA. Tell them how it happened. It's so romantic!

CONNIE. Wait, how come she already knows?

MARIO. *Are you insane!?*

ANTHONY. Mario, I know how you feel about…

MARIO. Andrew Polinski is the biggest player in Brooklyn. I have been telling you that for a year.

LUCIA. It's not your place, Mario.

MARIO. Yes, it is my place. I can't let Anthony do this. I'm his best friend, and I am going to be honest with him.

LUCIA. I love Andrew. He calls Anthony his little cinnabun.

MARIO. I just threw up in my mouth.

LUCIA. Get over it, Mario!

RODNEY. Yeah, Mario, now *ser tranquila y sentarse [hush up and sit down]*! You go with your badself, Anthony, baby. Now give Mommy kisses, *Loca.*

ANTHONY. Thank you, Rodney. Now the reason I invited you all here is because I would like all of you to be in my wedding party.

LUCIA. Get out! You didn't tell me that!

CONNIE. Guess you don't know everything, Miss Smarty-pants.

ANTHONY. And Mario…I would be very honored if you would stand up for me as my best man.

MARIO. Absolutely not.

ANTHONY. MARIO!

MARIO. No.

LUCIA. Mario, you're his best friend, how could you say no?

CONNIE. Look, if I have can deal with being in a bridal party with this bitch –

LUCIA. Do you ever come up for air?

RODNEY. Do we have to wear tuxes? They so don't work for me.

MARIA. I'm singing at the wedding!

ANTHONY. Everyone just hold it. Look, this is going to be the most important day of my life. I have finally found my soulmate and I am having a traditional Italian wedding that I want you all to be part of. *(to* **CONNIE & LUCIA***)* And those who are my friends will put their personal feelings aside *(to* **MARIO***)* and help me in creating this very special day.

MARIA. They will all do it, Anthony. Right?

FRANKIE. You know I'm in, babe.

RODNEY. Yes, and Frankie and I could pair up!

LUCIA. I would love to.

CONNIE. Well, I would love to more, so...

(They all look to **MARIO**.*)*

MARIO. Fine...even though you are making the biggest mistake of your life. I will be your best man.

*(***ANTHONY*** hugs him.)*

ANTHONY. Thank you!

LUCIA. So who is Andrew adding into the bridal party?

ANTHONY. No one. He really isn't close to a lot of people.

MARIO. That's 'cause he's slept with all of them.

MARIA. Does he even have a best man?

ANTHONY. I don't think he does.

FRANKIE. Let me ask you something, without getting too personal. How did you get your friggin' parents to throw you a wedding?

ANTHONY. Well, it wasn't easy, but they agreed.

MARIA. As long as Father Rosalia marries them and the Polish mother comes up from Florida to give her blessing.

ANTHONY. Exactly.

FRANKIE. You're screwed.

LUCIA. Frankie!

CONNIE. No, Frankie's right. Father Rosalia isn't going to marry you.

ANTHONY. Why not? I made the communion, confirmation...

FRANKIE. You're a fag; they won't do it.

ANTHONY. Well, I'll go in person to talk to him.

RODNEY. And what about Andrew's Momma? Does she know what's going on?

ANTHONY. No, but I'll just call her and tell her she has to come.

RODNEY. And if she doesn't...

ANTHONY. She will...

CONNIE. And if the priest says no...

ANTHONY. He won't....

MARIA. Anthony, you told Mommy you had everything under control...

ANTHONY. Everything is under control.

LUCIA. Sweetie, if your parents don't agree to throw you a wedding and Father Rosalia can't perform the service...you really should have a plan B.

RODNEY. Yeah, you could always have Mike Huckabee and Ann Colter throw you a wedding.

FRANKIE. And Laura Ingram can perform the service!

RODNEY. Sarah Palin might be available and at the reception Bristol Palin can do the Cha Cha!

FRANKIE. Nah, Sarah would just quit halfway through the ceremony.

(They crack up, amused at their own wit.)

LUCIA. Guys, would you be serious? Anthony is going to need his friends to help him to pull this off.

MARIO. Anthony is going to need a miracle to help him pull this off.

RODNEY. Gaymen to that, mister-sister. Anthony baby, start praying.

(They all look up.)

(blackout)

Scene IV
Regina Pacis Church

(A **NUN** *[ensemble] chants on the kneeler.)*

NUN. *Deus ex machina dominos pro bono nobis...E pluribus unum in utero targee....*

*(***ANDREW** *barrels in.)*

ANDREW. Sorry, sorry, we woke up late! Oh, guess I'm not late.

(The **NUN** *turns and glares at him.)*

NUN. Shhh!

ANDREW. Oh. Sorry, sister.

(The **NUN** *finishes her prayer and rises.)*

NUN. Amen.

ANDREW. I'm meeting some people here.

(The **NUN** *nods, then leaves.* **LUCIA** *and* **RODNEY** *enter.)*

LUCIA. Where's Anthony? Don't tell me he's still at home air-drying.

ANDREW. No, no, we came together. He's just wanted to run into the bakery next door.

LUCIA. What?! How can he think about pastries at a time like this?

RODNEY. Oh *mami*, I'm feeling bloated just thinking about it.

ANDREW. You look nice, Lucia.

LUCIA. Thank you.

*(***RODNEY** *clears his throat loudly.)*

ANDREW. You look nice too, Rodney.

RODNEY. Thank you, *chica.* Oh, Lucia, come here...

(He pulls a lipstick out of his own pocket and touches up her lips.)

Pucker, pucker, lips, hair, twirl around and throw your hands in the air! Now work it, own it, walk, then turn.

ANDREW. Lucia!

RODNEY. Show them that you mean it, baby! Burn, baby burn!

LUCIA. Wait in the car, Rodney.

RODNEY. I'll be in the bakery. BBM me and let me know how it's going!

(**RODNEY** *exits.*)

LUCIA. Mass ended a half hour ago. I hope we didn't miss him.

(**ANTHONY** *enters with the* **NUN** *wearing a not-so-appropriate outfit and carrying a box of cannolis.*)

ANTHONY. Lucia, thank God you're here! That god damn belt parkway had so much traffic!

(*The* **NUN** *clears her throat.* **ANTHONY** *misunderstands and takes out a twenty dollar bill.*)

ANTHONY. Oh, of course! I don't know what is wrong with me today. Thank you for your time, sister.

(*The* **NUN** *makes the sign of the cross and leaves.*)

LUCIA. I cannot believe you just tipped a nun.

ANTHONY. Oh Lucia, please, I see them in Atlantic City all the time.

LUCIA. And what are you wearing? This is a church, not *Dance Fever*! And what's with the pastries?

ANTHONY. Cannolis, fresh from Dominick's. I didn't want to come here with my arms swinging.

LUCIA. You're going to bribe a priest with cannolis? This will never work.

ANDREW. Be optimistic Lucia, you have big time connections with these people.

LUCIA. Oh yeah, me and the Pope, we do capuccino and cream puffs every Sunday. Are you nuts?

ANDREW. You said you go to church every Sunday!

LUCIA. Yeah, but Father Rosalia barely knows who I am. I bet he won't even recognize me.

(**FATHER ROSALIA** [*the favorite priest who is the crush of every parishioner, both male and female, and who tries hard to resist the temptations of the flesh, both male and female*] *enters.*)

FATHER ROSALIA. Lucia? Lucia Fuccio! Filomena and Giovanni's daughter. What a lovely surprise.

LUCIA. Good Afternoon, Father Rosalia.

FATHER ROSALIA. And your brother Luigi, how is he? He was my favorite altar boy.

LUCIA. He's good. I'm so sorry to bother you.

FATHER ROSALIA. Nonsense. Have a seat.

LUCIA. I actually came here with a huge favor to ask.

FATHER ROSALIA. What is the favor my child?

LUCIA. Well, I wanted to know if you could perform a wedding ceremony?

FATHER ROSALIA. Of course I can! What wonderful news! Let me get my calendar. Which one of you is the lucky man?

ANDREW. We both are father.

FATHER ROSALIA. Oh...oh....oh....I see. I see.

ANTHONY. Perhaps you may remember me? I'm Anthony Pinnunziato, Angela and Joseph's son. I was baptismed, communized, and confirmed all right here at Regina Pacis.

FATHER ROSALIA. Yes...oh yes, of course. How are your parents?

ANTHONY. Oh, they are blessed, Father, so blessed. Cannoli?

(**LUCIA** *steps in front of him.*)

LUCIA. So you see, Father Rosalia, Anthony and Andrew would like to get married in this church just like Anthony's parents were and –

FATHER ROSALIA. I can't.

ANDREW. Please, Father, this is so important to us.

FATHER ROSALIA. Same sex marriages are prohibited by the Catholic Church. I'm afraid even if I wanted to...I would still have to say no.

ANDREW. Thank you for your time, Father.

ANTHONY. Wait a minute! You don't understand; if you don't perform the ceremony my mother won't let me get married.

LUCIA. Calm down Anthony, not here.

ANTHONY. Father, I promise I'll cancel all my porn site subscriptions, I'll teach straight men how to moisturize, I'll even give up sex for Lent!

ANDREW. What?!

LUCIA. Anthony, stop!

ANTHONY. My convertible! You can have that too, my father just bought it for me a month ago, it's got 500 miles on it, not even!

(He drops to his knees in front of the priest.)

Whatever you want I'll do!

*(**FATHER ROSALIA** is affected by **ANTHONY**'s proximity and seems to consider for a moment.)*

FATHER ROSALIA. I'm sorry, Anthony, I just have to say no. Now, Mrs. Nicastro is here for her daily confession, I must go. God bless you.

*(**FATHER ROSALIA** makes sign of the cross, then exits, taking the pastries with him.)*

ANDREW. Well, now what?

LUCIA. I knew this wouldn't work.

ANDREW. All right, I'm sure we can figure something out. Maybe if you try and explain to your mother...

ANTHONY. Have you met my mother?

LUCIA. Speaking of mothers...

ANDREW. Oh...yeah...my mother.

ANTHONY. Did you call her?

ANDREW. Well...

LUCIA. What are you waiting for?

ANDREW. For his mother to forget about my mother?

ANTHONY. She's not going to, can you please just call her and just tell her she has to come?

ANDREW. She's not going to say yes.

ANTHONY. Give me the phone.

(**ANTHONY** *grabs Andrew's cell phone from* **ANDREW**.)

Is she programmed in here?

ANDREW. Yes, but she's not going to say yes to me.

ANTHONY. Well, then maybe she will say yes to me.

LUCIA. Anthony, you've lost your mind. This woman is going to think you're insane.

(**ANTHONY** *dials.*)

ANDREW. If the shoe fits.

LUCIA. Maybe it will be ok. Mothers love him.

ANTHONY. Hello, Mrs. Polinski. How are you? My name is Anthony Pinnunziato, I'm a friend of Andrew's. Yes, he's fine...everything is fine...Well, I was actually calling to tell you that he's getting married...to me, Anthony, and he would love to have you at the wedding....Hello? Hello? Mrs. Polinski, Mrs. Polinski... Can you hear me?

(*He takes a few steps looking for reception.*)

Can you hear me now? We got disconnected. I'll call her back...

ANDREW. She hung up.

ANTHONY. Why would she do that?

ANDREW. She doesn't accept my being gay, what made you think she would want me to get married?

LUCIA. Looks to me like you're not getting married anyway. Mrs. Pinnunziato will never allow this.

(**ANTHONY** *starts to cry.*)

ANDREW. All right, calm down, we can figure something out

LUCIA. Maybe you should just elope.

(ANTHONY *cries more.*)

ANTHONY. Elope!? ELOPE!! Excuse me...

ANDREW. Where are you going?

ANTHONY. I want my cannolis back.

(ANTHONY *exits.*)

LUCIA. You know, now that I think about it. It would only be one time that anyone would ever have to see your mother, Andrew. I mean, after all...she does live in Florida. She could be anybody!

ANDREW. What are you saying?

LUCIA. I'm saying that I think we both know someone who could fit the role. And well.

ANDREW. We do?

LUCIA. Come on, who's the girliest mother hen you know?

ANDREW. Uh, well, Rodney, but –

LUCIA. Exactly!

ANDREW. What? He's Cuban!

LUCIA. Venezuelan.

ANDREW. Whatever! My mother's Polish!

LUCIA. Well, we'll just say she lives by a beach. Trust me, no one will notice.

ANDREW. Do you really think that will work?

LUCIA. It will have to.

ANDREW. Ok, then what about the priest?

LUCIA. That part's easy. I'm sure we can find a minister online.

ANDREW. But his mother wants Father Rosalia.

LUCIA. Enough with Father Rosalia! Don't worry, I have a plan.

ANDREW. Ok. Well, then I guess it will all work out. Right?

LUCIA. Right.

ANDREW. I'd better go get him.

(ANDREW *exits,* LUCIA *crosses to the kneeler and prays.*)

LUCIA. Are you there God? It's me, Lucia Margharita Bernadette Fuccio, Catholic. Please let this go well for Anthony. He's a good boy. He deserves to be happy. He just wants to get married like everyone else does. I know some people think it's a big deal and don't want to support him, but deep down I know that you're okay with this. So please, help us. Thank you. I mean, Amen.

(blackout)

Scene V
Bacci's Foyer

(**ANGELA**, **MARIA** and **AUNT TONIANN** *cross in front of the closed curtain, on their way to the rehearsal hall.*)

ANGELA. I still have so much to do before tomorrow. I have to take the plastic slipcovers off the sofa, I have to pick up the almond favors...And I don't know what I'm doing with my hair. I don't care what Louise, Joanne, or any of the other girls from the bowling alley say, this new hairdresser in Dolce Salon, sucks! Look at my hair; it's way too flat!

MARIA. Mine too! Aunt Toniann, does this look high enough to you?

AUNT TONIANN. Well, you know what I always say, the higher the hair...the closer to God.

(She takes out Aqua Net and starts to fix all their hair do's.)

So yous gonna let me finish my story or what?

ANGELA. *Madonna!* You're still on the same story! I've been hearing this story since nine o'clock this morning

TONIANN. Well, if you would stop interrupting me, and let me finish...

MARIA. I want to hear it!

(**ANGELA** *rolls her eyes.* **TONIANN** *turns to her niece, who hangs on her every word.*)

TONIANN. So, I'm with Baby Anna and Ro Ro, and we're walking back toward the restaurant at the Borgata because you know Ro Ro, God forbid she tries something new, she's so frigging picky. Anyway, I pass a Wheel Of Fortune slot machine and I get a vibe.... almost like a little chill like the one you get when you get a déjà vu? And there is a Chinese man who is just getting up and Angela, remember how *Papa* always used to say the Chinese people were good luck...

*(Enter **JOSEPH** on his cell phone.)*

MARIA. Oh, here comes Daddy!

JOSEPH. Gimme five hundred on Lucky Lady to place first. Would you stop nagging me about the odds! I know what they are! Speaking of nags, I gotta go.

ANGELA. What happened with the cake?

JOSEPH. I took care of it.

ANGELA. You went to Dominick's in Staten Island?

JOSEPH. Yeah, he said it's all good.

ANGELA. How big of a cake did you get?

JOSEPH. I told him six hundred people.

ANGELA. Joseph, we're only three hundred!

JOSEPH. What if everybody wants two pieces?!

TONIANN. You just want the leftovers for yourself.

JOSEPH. Hey Toniann, you did your hair?

AUNT TONIANN. Yeah.

JOSEPH. It sucks.

AUNT TONIANN. Well at least my hair didn't slip off my head and land on my ass.

(**MARIA** *jumps in before the argument can escalate.*)

MARIA. So Aunt Toniann, what happened to the Chinese man?

AUNT TONIANN. Oh right. So I'm by the slot machines....

ANGELA. Finish telling us later or we're gonna be late, let's go inside.

AUNT TONIANN. But I didn't get to the best part....

(*They cross over and greet* **ANDREW, FRANKIE, MARIO, LUCIA,** *and* **CONNIE,** *who are already inside.* **CONNIE** *and* **LUCIA** *are sitting far away from each other.* **ANTHONY,** *carrying two different portraits, comes down stage frantic to* **LUCIA.**)

ANTHONY. Lucia, thank God you're here! I'm a nervous wreck. What do you think, should Andrew and I wear the white tuxedos, or the black ones?

LUCIA. Wear the white one Anthony and let Andrew wear the black one, he's more butch.

(CONNIE *overhears.*)

CONNIE. No, no, no. First off, you don't go taking fashion tips from Snookie over here. And two, yous both wear the black because that's traditional. And besides you're just as butch as he is.

LUCIA. Well, Connie would definitely know what butch is. After all she left me for a woman who made Chaz Bono look like Angelina Jolie.

CONNIE. I'll have you know that Gianna was almost a contestant on America's Next Top Model.

LUCIA. Really? Cause from your Facebook photo, she looks like she could be a contestant for The Biggest Loser!

CONNIE. Oh! So you're stalking my Facebook, huh, you jealous bitch!? Missing what you can't have?

(CONNIE *pushes* LUCIA *and then* LUCIA *lunges at* CONNIE, *knocking* ANTHONY *into* MARIO *and* FRANKIE.)

MARIO. Oh my God, you can't take lesbians anywhere.

FRANKIE. *Basta!* Do yous two ever stop?

CONNIE. I'm sorry, Anthony. If you need anything else just come to me first, baby doll.

(LUCIA *bites her fists to hold back as* CONNIE *saunters off.* ANTHONY's *cell phone rings.*)

ANTHONY. Hi, Mom. Yes, we're all here, we're all inside. Well, what are you doing outside? Tell Aunt Toniann to put out the cigarette and come inside.

(ANDREW *motions to her and they pull* FRANKIE *aside.*)

ANDREW. Frankie, could we talk to you?

FRANKIE. What's up?

LUCIA. What do you think of Rodney?

FRANKIE. Isn't he supposed to be here?

ANDREW. He's not going to be in the bridal party any more.

LUCIA. He's going to be dressing up as Andrew's mother.

FRANKIE. Whoa! That's serious shit!

ANDREW. We made a deal with him so Anthony's mother won't pull the plug on the whole wedding.

FRANKIE. A deal? But, how's that gonna work, he's like Argentinean.

LUCIA & ANDREW. Venezuelan.

FRANKIE. Whatever. Look, I've seen this on Jerry Springer… it ain't gonna work.

ANDREW. We have to make it work. There's no other option.

FRANKIE. Okay. But what does any of this have to do with me?

LUCIA. That's where the whole 'deal' part comes in.

ANDREW. He said he would do it in exchange for a date with you.

FRANKIE. ME?! Why me?

LUCIA. You know he's been crushing on you forever.

ANDREW. Come on, it could be your wedding present to me and Anthony.

FRANKIE. I can't believe Anthony is going along with this.

LUCIA. He doesn't know about it yet.

ANDREW. He can't know, he'd freak out. Let this be one less thing for him to worry about, please?

FRANKIE. What are you my mother with this guilt?

LUCIA. Have you been working out?

ANDREW. Oh, wow…

FRANKIE. All right, I'll do it. I guess Rodney isn't so bad.

ANDREW. Thanks, Frankie.

LUCIA. Thanks so much, Frankie. Group hug!

(They hug. CONNIE is visibly annoyed.)

FRANKIE. Yeah, yeah. So listen, it's your present, you know you ain't getting an envelope.

(AUNT TONIANN rises, looks around, and spots LUCIA.)

TONIANN. Lucia! How gorgeous you look today!

CONNIE. Toniann, did you leave your glasses in the car?

LUCIA. Thank you, Aunt Toniann! Oh look Connie, the pastry cart.

(CONNIE gives her the finger and walks off.)

TONIANN. Did your cousin Roe Roe tell you we went down to AC last night?

LUCIA. No, I haven't talked to her.

TONIANN. Oh my God! Funny story, come here. There's this Chinese man…

(She pulls her by the arm.)

MARIA. Ma, I thought you hired a wedding coordinator?

ANGELA. I did. He should have been here by now.

MARIA. Who'd you get?

ANGELA. You ready for this…I got Maurizio LeGrande.

MARIA. Oh my God, I just saw a story on him on TMZ! I can't believe you got him!

ANGELA. Anthony will be so surprised!

(From offstage a high-pitched voice is heard.)

MAURIZIO. *(offstage)* Yoo hoo! Is this the right place? I never leave Manhattan…Is this Bacci's? Do I hear the sound of two gay boys in love?

(MAURIZIO LEGRANDE [outlandishly dressed, over the top and flamboyant wedding coordinator with an accent that can't be pegged down] makes his grand late entrance.)

So sorry I'm late. Traffic galore.

ANTHONY. Maurizio LeGrande!

MAURIZIO. Guilty!

FRANKIE. Holy Mother of Mary, you're the wedding coordinator? Yo, I'm Frankie. How you doing?

(LUCIA leaves TONIANN and runs over to ANTHONY.)

LUCIA. Oh my God! Didn't he do Heidi and Seal's wedding?

MAURIZIO. My time is very valuable people so let us begin right away shall we. Who are the grooms?

ANTHONY & ANDREW. We are!

MAURIZIO. Fabulous gay couple! The last gay wedding I did was my own.

AUNT TONIANN. He's gay?

MAURIZIO. Needless to say it was totally flawless. We can try to do the same for you two.

ANTHONY. Thank you so much….

MAURIZIO. No talking! No talking! Now I assume this is the bridal party.

(He points to **ANTHONY.***)*

Who is your best man?

MARIO. That would be me.

*(***MAURIZIO** *goes over to check him out at every angle.)*

MAURIZIO. Yummy yummy. Who's a pretty girl? Who's a pretty girl?

MARIO. Me? Me!

MAURIZIO. Fabulous. And you Mr. Polinoscopy?

ANDREW. Polinsky. And I don't have one.

*(***GREGORIO** *enters.)*

GREGORIO. Yes, you do! So sorry I'm late everyone. I'm Gregorio, Andrew's best friend. We go back a long way. Right, Drew?

ANTHONY. What a pleasure to meet you!

GREGORIO. You must be *Ant'* - Anthony. I heard so much about you.

*(***MARIO** *pulls* **FRANKIE** *aside.)*

MARIO. He looks so familiar.

FRANKIE. I call dibs. He's hot!

MAURIZIO. Hi! How are you? How are you? I'm a Capricorn, I love long walks on the beach…intro's later! Time is money, people, money is time. Any more surprises? Is the flower girl going to come flying in from the ceiling?

MARIA. Oooh! Ma!?

(**ANGELA** *shakes her head.* **MARIA** *is crushed.*)

MAURIZIO. Okay good…now let's discuss the ceremony. I'm thinking organza. Oraganza, organza, organza –

MARIA. I'm gonna sing at the ceremony!

MAURIZIO. I am so excited!…And who might you be?

MARIA. Maria.

(**MAURIZIO** *stares at her blankly.*)

Pinnunziato.

(**MAURIZIO** *makes a sound like a buzzer.*)

MAURIZIO. Play again.

MARIA. Anthony's sister?

MAURIZIO. Oh! Oh! Yes, of course! And what will you be singing my little cherub?

MARIA. The Ave…Maria! Get it? The Ave….MARIA!

MAURIZIO. Oh yes, because that is your name and that is the name of the song and how do you solve a problem like Maria?

(*He forcefully sits her back down.*)

ANGELA. Mr. Le Grande, it's traditional for a family member to sing during the ceremony.

MAURIZIO. Well, Cher sang at my wedding, but that was far from traditional.

(**MARIA** *jumps up from her chair.*)

MARIA. Everyone says I sound just like Cher!

(**MARIA** *belts out an awful rendition of a [producer's choice] song. Finally,* **MAURIZIO** *can't take it and stops her.*)

MAURIZIO. Stop it! Cut! Cut! Oh that is so wonderful but let's save that for your debut on American Idol!

(*He forcefully sits her down again.*)

Stay in your chair, Cher… Now, you. Who is going to give you away?

ANTHONY. My mother.

(**AUNT TONIANN** *holds* **ANGELA** *for support.*)

MAURIZIO. I love it. Cut, print. And you Mister Poland Springs?

ANDREW. Polinski. And I haven't really thought…

MAURIZIO. Will your mother be attending the service?

ANDREW. Uh…yes.

MAURIZIO. Excellent, where is she?

ANDREW. She flies in the day of the service.

MAURIZIO. She will give you away then.

ANDREW. But…

MAURIZIO. Don't "but" me, Mr. Groom Person! The mothers will give away their sons it will look *Vunderbar.* Now, who will be performing the service?

ANGELA. Father Rosalia.

AUNT TONIANN. He agreed?

ANTHONY. Yup, he agreed.

MAURIZIO. And where is he?

(**ANDREW** *shoots* **LUCIA** *a pointed look.*)

ANDREW. He must be running late.

(**LUCIA** *takes her cue and hides in a corner to call Anthony's cell phone.*)

MAURIZIO. Late! That's unacceptable. I can't work like this. How can we do a proper rehearsal without him –

(**ANTHONY**'*s cell phone rings.*)

ANTHONY. Oh this must be him. Hello….oh yes, hello Father Rosalia, where are you?

ANGELA. He's probably parking the car.

ANTHONY. Kidney stones?

(**MAURIZIO** *sits and begins to fan himself impatiently.*)

ANGELA. WHAT?! Oh my God! Maria, Toniann, get me a chair!

(*She collapses into the chair.*)

ANTHONY. You're not going to be able to perform the service!

(ANGELA *jumps up and tries to grab the phone.*)

ANGELA. Let me talk to him!

ANTHONY. Well, get well soon. That was Father Rosalia. He said he has to have immediate surgery but there's good news. We got Pastor Bosco –

ANGELA. Who?

ANTHONY. Pastor Bosco, who is a, um…

ANGELA. Chocolate drink?

ANTHONY. No! Umm, he's a….a…

ANDREW. A Unitarian Pastor!

ANTHONY. Yes! Yes, a Unitarian Pastor.

ANGELA. From where?

(ANTHONY, *flustered, looks to* LUCIA *and* ANDREW, *who pantomimes the answers to him.*)

ANTHONY. Umm…I'm totally blanking…he's from that nice place, it's very hot there…where old people roam?… Florida!

ANGELA. What church?

ANTHONY. What church? Oh, you know that church, ummm…Our Lady Queen of the Pigeons.

ANGELA. What?

ANTHONY. Uh, Angels! Yes, that's it. Our Lady Queen of the Angels. *That* Pastor Bosco will be performing the service instead.

ANGELA. He got who…from where…to do what? I need to sit down.

AUNT TONIANN. You know Angela, we really should send flowers to Father Rosalia.

ANGELA. I never even heard of Pastor Bosco. Where is this Floridian Unitarian Pastor person?

ANTHONY. He will be here for the service.

(MAURIZIO *stands, fed up.*)

MAURIZIO. For the love of God can we please get started! My God this is a weird family. The Pope himself can drive here all the way from the Vatican in his bullet-proof Pope-mobile and perform the service, I don't give a shit!

(He snaps and points to **FRANKIE.***)*

Goomba, get my bag! I'm having dinner with Michael Kors and Tim Gunn and I need to get home and fluff first. Oh my, aren't you a big Italian sausage?

*(***MAURIZIO*** leaps into* **FRANKIE***'s arms.)*

Everyone follow me into the larger room. Because size matters people! Chop Chop!

(They all exit, except **MARIO,** *who stops* **GREGORIO.***)*

MARIO. Hey, do I know you from somewhere?

GREGORIO. I don't think so.

MARIO. Oh jeez, that wasn't a line. You just look kinda familiar.

*(***GREGORIO*** considers a moment.)*

GREGORIO. Yes. Splash. About five years ago. We met there…had a few drinks…Those guys walked in on us in the bathroom…

MARIO. Oh God, that's right! You know, I never do things like that.

GREGORIO. Um hmmm.

MARIO. No, seriously, I am so not like that! Could you please do me a favor and not mention it to anyone. It would be so embarrassing!

*(***ANDREW*** re-enters, looking for* **GREGORIO.***)*

ANDREW. Hey Mario, you should really go help Anthony and his mother pick out the linen colors.

MARIO. Oh, God. Please don't tell me he is still trying to pair the mauve napkins with the burgundy tablecloths!

*(***MARIO*** dashes off to stop the fashion nightmare.)*

GREGORIO. I sure hope I don't have to dance with that little queen at the reception.

ANDREW. That would be impossible, since you won't be there.

GREGORIO. Of course I will! I'm your best man! Why don't you pair me off with that hot Frankie guy. I think I'll give him my number before the rehearsal starts.

ANDREW. Damn it, Gregorio! What the hell are you doing here?

GREGORIO. Ummm...rehearsing? Don't want to give you the rings at the wrong time. Or speak when I should be holding my peace.

ANDREW. I knew it.

(**MARIO** *renters, sees the confrontation, and ducks back to spy, his curiosity getting the better of him.*)

GREGORIO. What? You think I came here to tell Anthony what a lying, cheating player you are?

ANDREW. He won't believe anything you say.

GREGORIO. Really? We'll see –

ANDREW. What do you want?

GREGORIO. All I want is to be here for you. To be your best man. That's all.

ANDREW. Really. That's all. I let you be my best man, and you don't blow everything up and make a big scene about what happened in Fire Island.

GREGORIO. Exactly. I just want to be respected. I want you to treat me like a friend and not some trick you had Memorial Day Weekend.

ANDREW. I can't believe this is happening.

GREGORIO. Oh, stop Andrew. This will be fun! I'm actually looking forward to it.

(**GREGORIO** *looks at his watch.*)

Now, as much as I would love to help look at linens and talk arrangements, I have a date. But I will be all ready and here for you tomorrow. Ciao Ciao!

(**GREGRIO** *leaves and* **ANDREW** *heads off to the rehearsal.* **MARIO** *steps out of concealment, stunned at what he has overheard. He does the sign of the cross – with the wrong hand.*)

MARIO. Jesus, take the wheel!

End Act One

ACT TWO

Bacci's Wedding Hall

*(While a [producer's choice] song plays, **MAURIZIO LEGRANDE** enters front and center, checking that all is ready. He then cues the music to change to the wedding processional music, "Canon in D," and directs the bridal party to begin entering. If possible, the procession moves through the audience and onto the stage.)*

*(**MARIA** enters first as the flower girl, throwing rose petals down the aisle. Next come **CONNIE** and **LUCIA**, forcing smiles, but their animosity for each other can't help but be noticeable.)*

CONNIE. What the hell are you wearing?

LUCIA. The same thing you're wearing.

CONNIE. Oh, yeah.

*(Following them is **FRANKIE**, whose cell phone rings. He answers.)*

FRANKIE. No, I can't talk, I'm walking down the aisle. Yeah, right now…Ma…MA!…I gotta go! Okay…okay…. Yeah, I'll tell him you said hi.

*(Next comes **MARIO**, alone, weepy but not with happiness. Finally, **GREGORIO** with a canary eating grin.)*

*(**MAURIZIO** cues the music and "Here Comes the Bride" begins to play. **MAURIZIO** address the audience.)*

MAURIZIO. Stand up people! Stand up!

*(Down the aisle comes **ANDREW**, with **RODNEY**, who is now dressed as his version of Mrs. Polinski, in an outlandish gown, wig, and makeup. Everyone in the bridal party is immediately aware that it's **RODNEY** and break out into hysterical laughter.)*

*(Next comes **ANTHONY** and **ANGELA**. As **ANGELA** walks down the aisle she smiles and waves at audience members, thanks them for coming, and berates others for wearing jeans or other inappropriate clothes to her son's wedding. **ANTHONY** tries to shush and calm her.)*

*(**ANGELA** brings **ANTHONY** to the stage and gives her son a kiss. **ANTHONY** gets his first look at Andrew's 'mother' and tries to cover his shock. Then **ANGELA** turns and spots "Mrs. Polinski" for the first time and the smile freezes on her face. "**MRS. POLINSKI**" (**RODNEY**) waves hello.)*

"MRS. POLINSKI" (RODNEY). Hey.

*(**MAURIZIO** gestures for everone to sit. As they do, everyone looks around in silence. There is an awkward moment as everyone wonders where the pastor is. **ANGELA** is temporarily distracted by Mrs. Polinski but then she finally snaps to.)*

ANGELA. Anthony, I'm two seconds from a nervous breakdown. Where is this Floridian Pastor!? Tell him to get this thing going before I have a stroke!

ANTHONY. I…I…I don't know…Andrew?

ANDREW. Lucia…do you have his number?

LUCIA. I didn't have anywhere to put my phone!

CONNIE. I'll tell you where you can put your fucking phone.

MAURIZIO. I have the number and I have the fucking phone. *(aside to **CONNIE**)* Nice. *(to all)* Part of being the wedding coordinator is being prepared in case of emergencies.

(He takes out his phone and dials the pastor.)

Hello, is this Pastor Bosco of the Unitarian Floridian Flying Episcopalians? This is Maurizio Legrande, of the Palm Beach and Minneola LeGrandes. Aren't you supposed to be performing a service for – You missed your flight!

ANGELA. Oh my God! Joseph!

MAURIZIO. Well, when were you going to let me know?...
Oh, you texted the Best Man?

(He looks at **MARIO**, *who checks his phone and finds nothing.)*

MARIO. Lies.

*(***MAURIZIO*** then glares pointedly at* **GREGORIO**, *who makes a show of looking at his cell phone as if for the first time.)*

GREGORIO. Sorry, it was on vibrate.

MAURIZIO. No, don't bother re-booking. You're fired.

*(***MAURIZIO*** hangs up.* **GREGORIO** *reads the text.)*

GREGORIO. "Missed flight. My bad. Please call."

ANTHONY. Now what?

MARIO. I guess you'll have to postpone.

JOSEPH. Nobody's postponing nothing.

(He points to **MAURIZIO**.*)*

You. Liberace. Fix this. Now.

MAURIZIO. Calm down, papa guido, today is your lucky day.
Moi just happens to be a bonafide, certified, sanctified,
minister.

LUCIA. What!?

AUNT TONIANN. Get the Hell outta here!?

MAURIZIO. Yes, I received my certificate online at Merry
Minister dot Org. So I can marry happy gay boys
myself! For a small, additional fee, of course.

JOSEPH. Of course.

MAURIZIO. Ten thousand. Up front.

JOSEPH. Are you kidding me?

ANGELA. Joseph, just write him a check.

MAURIZIO. Cash.

JOSEPH. I ain't got that kind of cash on me! What are you,
nuts?

MAURIZIO. No cash, no wedding ceremony...

LUCIA. Mister LeGrande please, he's obviously good for it!

TONIANN. Oh would you stop already, I got it!

(**TONIANN** *whips out her larger-than-life pocketbook and takes out a wad of cash.*)

JOSEPH. Where did you get all that money?!

TONIANN. I hit the jackpot in AC!

ANGELA. What!? And when were you gonna tell me this?

TONIANN. Well, maybe if you would let me finish a story. That's your wedding present Anthony. I'm the Godmother!

MAURIZIO. I'm so happy we worked that out. Thank you Fairy Godmother. Now, shall we begin? Dearly Beloved, we are here to join these two happy happy gay boys in the sacrament of marriage. These two happy, happy, gay, gay, boys are in love…so in love that they want to spend their whole happy, happy, gay, gay, lives together, forever, as one. Now at this time…we have a *special* song…ahhh…and if you need to use the powder room, this would be a good time for that too. Sixteen bars Maria. Go!

(*Everyone braces themselves for the worst but* **MARIA** *surprises them all with a fabulous rendition of the first part of the "Ave Maria." Everyone applauds.**)

MARIA.

AVE MARIA GRATIA PLENA,

MARIA GRATIA PLENA,

MARIA GRATIA PLENA.

AVE AVE DOMINUS.

DOMINUS TE-CUM.

MAURIZIO. My dear, that was…*good.*

MARIA. Wait, here comes the best part.

(*Suddenly the traditional song is turned into a modernized, punkified version, which takes things just a little too far.*)

---

*Please see "A Note About the Music" on Page 4.

MARIA. *(cont.)*

WHEN I SAY HAIL, YOU SAY MARY

HAIL, (MARY)

HAIL (MARY)

WHEN I SAY AVE, YOU SAY MARIA

AVE (MARIA)

AVE (MARIA)

MARIA THAT'S MY NAME, THAT'S MY NAME

HAIL MARY THAT'S MY GAME, THAT'S MY GAME

AVE

AVE

AND YOU - HA!

AND YOU - HA!

AND YOU

YOU'RE GONNA LOVE ME!

*(**MAURIZIO** cuts her off.)*

MAURIZIO. Sorry! Outta time, my little One Hit Wonder. Never in my entire life have I squeezed my butt cheeks together that tightly. Thank you, Maria.

(He prods her back to her seat.)

Let's continue, yes....? I understand that our two grooms will be reciting their own vows to each other. Ummmm...you. You start.

ANTHONY. Andrew....the night I met you I felt like the whole world stopped. You came up to me in the middle of a bar and with those big beautiful (green) eyes you looked right at me and said, "Are you on Facebook?" You smiled and I laughed, and then we both laughed together and we've been laughing together ever since. That's all I want....that's all I've ever wanted more than anything in the world is someone to laugh with, someone to love with and someone to grow with. And till death do us part I want to do all of that with you.

(ANTHONY starts to cry. CONNIE and LUCIA both try to get him a tissue, struggling to see who can hand it to him first. Everyone else starts to applaud.)

MAURIZIO. Awww…that was so sweet. Now –

ANTHONY. Wait, no…one more thing. I have a confession to make Andrew, right before we met, I went to see a psychic…

(He turns to the audience.)

…Francesca Bucculato on eighteenth avenue. My cousin Rosanna –

(He waves to an audience member.)

– said she was the best around and Rosanna, you were right. Francesca told me that I was going to marry the man who comforts me when something bad happens. Andrew the night we met I don't know if you even remember because we were totally wasted, but on our first date at Feathers, I had just got a text from Connie Scuccifuffio that our good friend Angela Suppa Pagnotta was moving all the way to Connecticut and I was devastated. But you knew, you knew how upset I was, and then almost like an angel you came and you found me and you comforted me outside the stall of the men's room while I was peeing. I will never forget that.

(MARIA, AUNT TONIANN, and ANGELA all burst out into tears at the same time. All start to applaud.)

MAURIZIO. Okaaaaay. Moving right along –

ANTHONY. Wait! One more thing, one more thing. In case I never told you before, I love you, Andrew Polinski. And nothing will ever change that.

(ANDREW is dumbfounded and very taken by his words. No one applauds.)

ANTHONY. I'm done.

MAURIZIO. Fabulous!

(All applaud.)

Now you go. In thirty seconds or less please.

(ANDREW looks to GREGORIO knowing he better keep this simple.)

ANDREW. Anthony, I love you and no matter what happens just remember that...I love you.

(GREGORIO cringes.)

MAURIZIO. Excellent! Moving on...

(ANGELA rises, animalistic. AUNT TONIANN tries to calm her.)

ANGELA. That's it? That's all your gonna say to my son, after he pours his heart out to you???

ANTHONY. Ma!

TONIANN. Calm down Angela! He's Polish.

ANTHONY. Andrew doesn't need to say any more. His actions speak louder than anything he could possibly say.

MARIO. They speak volumes.

(ANDREW looks to MARIO and then GREGORIO wondering if he told.)

ANDREW. You're right, Mario. They do. And my actions for the rest of my life will prove every day just how much I love Anthony. You have changed my whole life. Before I met you, I was pretty lost. I went from party to party, and guy to guy, and inside I was absolutely miserable. And then I met you, and you smiled at me, and everything changed. I'm a better man when I'm with you, and I love you like I've never loved anyone else. You really are the love of my life.

MAURIZIO. Well said, my lovelys! And now we move on to my favorite part, the rings. Show me some bling people!

(Nothing happens. He hits MARIO off the head.)

MAURIZIO. Ding bat! That was your cue! See if you weren't texting during the rehearsal like a sixteen year-old girl you would have remembered. Now we are completely behind my schedule! Blessed these rings O Lord...O Lord...O Lord...*(he bursts into his own made up song:)* Rays of Sun, Rays of Sun, Baby Jesus...Holy! Holy! Jingle Bells! Jingle Bells! And now they are blessed. Okay, place this ring on his finger and repeat after me. "With this ring I thee wed."

ANTHONY. "With this ring I thee wed."

MAURIZIO. Now you, place this ring on his finger and say "With this ring I thee wed."

ANDREW. "With this ring I thee wed."

MAURIZIO. Anthony, do you take him –

ANTHONY. I DO!!

MAURIZIO. The short version. I like it. How about you?

ANDREW. Um, yes.

MAURIZIO. Are you sure?

ANDREW. Yes!

MAURIZIO. Positive?

ANDREW. YES!!

MAURIZIO. Then say "I Do," Dum Dum.

ANDREW. I do, dum dum!

MAURIZIO. Okay. What's next? We did the rings, we did the vows, we did the songs –

(GREGORIO leans over and whispers in his ear)

Oh, right! If anyone here has any reason why these two men should not be joined together, speak now or forever hold your peace.

(GREGORIO starts to speak but MARIO sees.)

GREGORIO. Ladies and –

MARIO. Oh my God! I don't feel so good.

(MARIO pretends to faint. FRANKIE and LUCIA run to help him help him get back on his feet. Then MAURIZIO pushes everyone out of the way to get to MARIO.)

MAURIZIO. Everyone out of the way, I was a girl scout!

(He sees he is faking.)

Oh my goodness, look at his package!

*(**MARIO** bolts up.)*

MARIO. Where?

MAURIZIO. You're faking! Get back to your place! Everyone back to your places. You are the Worst Man. The Worst Man! Now, I believe the other best man was about to say something?

*(**GREGORIO** steps forward, **ANTHONY** is pleasantly surprised while **MARIO** and **ANDREW** are completely thunderstruck. **GREGORIO** sashays his way to the front and looks to **ANDREW**, teasing him at all moments, making him wonder if he is going to reveal the truth.)*

GREGORIO. Ladies and Gents, I wanted to say a few words because I've known Andrew longer than anyone here, aside from his lovely mother, of course.

*(He gallantly kisses **MRS. POLINKSY**'s hand.)*

"MRS. POLINSKY." Okay...

GREGORIO. I want to assure Anthony's whole family that Andrew is a gem. It's true that he used to be a wild party boy, but those days are long over. He would never do anything to hurt Anthony or betray his trust, in any way. Andrew, I hope today is one that you will remember for the rest of your life, and I hope that you get everything you deserve.

(He goes back to his spot.)

MAURIZIO. Anyone else ? No? No one else wants to give a long, boring speech that makes me want to gouge my eyes out with a spoon?

(He points to an audience member.)

You down there? You in the _____ *(actor calls out a feature of the audience member).* You look like you want to say something. No? Okay! We are getting married today and we are way way behind schedule so....by the powers in my vest, and by the authority of W-W-W-dot-find-a-minister-dot-com-slash-gov-slash-org, I now pronounce this happy gay couple husband and husband! Now make out like you mean it!

(They kiss as wedding closing music begins to play. **MARIO** *and* **LUCIA** *cry their eyes out with* **ANGELA** *and* **AUNT TONIANN.** **MAURIZIO** *steps up ushering everyone out, until he's the only one left on stage. Another [producer's choice] song plays to establish the transition from church to reception hall.* **MAURIZIO** *is still center stage and welcomes everyone. A light change, and tables come out to help create the transition from wedding ceremony to reception.)*

MAURIZIO. *(cont.)* Good evening, everyone! Are we gonna have fun tonight?! Of course we are, because we are all here to celebrate the wedding of Anthony Pinnatta and Andrew Polloloco. I just can't say the name! *(To audience member:)* Do you know how to do the Italian Booty Shake? Well, you are about to find out. Now without any further hesitation…the fabulous, stunning bridal party!

("Italian Booty Shake" plays as **LUCIA, MARIA,** *and* **CONNIE** *come out to a choreographed portion of the song. Then* **MARIO, FRANKIE,** *and* **GREGORIO** *take over.*)*

Fabulous! Let's hear it for the Bridal Party!

*(***FRANKIE** *body slams* **MAURIZIO.***)*

Frankie, what did I tell you about when I am wearing the couture. And now ladies and gentleman, I present to you for the first time as Husband and Husband, Anthony and Andrew! And now the happy gay couple will attempt to dance to their happy gay wedding song.

---

* Please see a "A Note About the Music" on page 4

("Love Conquers All" begins to play as **ANTHONY** *and* **ANDREW** *come into a spotlight and dance.* **MAURIZIO** *occasionally calls out choreography "reminders." Eventually everyone else joins them. When the song finishes,* **ANTHONY** *and* **ANDREW** *continue to slow dance.*)*

MARIO. I know what you were trying to do, and I'm not going to let you do it.

GREGORIO. Oh? And what was I trying to do?

MARIO. Don't play dumb. I heard you talking to Andrew, and I know all about your little fling.

GREGORIO. Really? Then why haven't you run off to tattle tales to your little BFF? Martini.

(A **BARTENDER** *[ensemble] makes him a drink.)*

MARIO. Oh don't worry, I'll tell him what's going on. But not here, not in front of all these people.

GREGORIO. So that's what that little fainting stunt was about.

MARIO. I'm not going to let you embarrass Anthony and ruin this day for him.

GREGORIO. Oh back off, drama queen! Threaten me again and watch what happens!

*(***GREGORIO** *then steps away and grabs a drink off a table, then deliberately trips into* **ANTHONY**, *knocking the drink all over him.* **ANTHONY** *runs to* **AUNT TONI-ANN** *to wipe up the mess.* **ANDREW** *grabs* **GREGORIO**, *who eggs him on. Then* **ANDREW** *thinks better of it and pushes him away, and goes over to* **ANTHONY**.*)*

Sorry!

ANTHONY. Oh it's fine. Aunt Toniann!

TONIANN. Oh Jesus! Club soda! Connie, get me club soda and salt right away!

---

*Please see a "A Note About the Music" on page 4

(ANGELA and JOSEPH are still dancing. ANGELA suddenly notices that MRS. POLINSKI is completely alone.)

ANGELA. Oh look, Joseph, Mrs. Polinski has no one to dance with. Go dance with her.

JOSEPH. Of course I will.

(TONIANN continues to work aggressively on the stain.)

TONIANN. I got that Tide To Go stick. Maria, my bag.

(JOSEPH goes over to "MRS. POLINSKI.")

Mrs. Polinski, would you like to dance?

(RODNEY has been drinking heavily and in a very high-pitched voice delivers his version of a Polish accent.)

"MRS POLINSKY." Oh! Da! Da!

(They start to dance. AUNT TONIANN is now using hairspray on the stain. ANTHONY decides it's good enough and goes back to the dance floor with ANDREW.)

ANTHONY. Are you nuts? I can't believe you dressed up Rodney as your mother! He's not even Polish!

ANDREW. No one knows he's Columbian.

ANTHONY. Venezuelan.

ANDREW. Whatever. It's working perfectly. Look at him, he's doing great.

ANTHONY. Oh yeah, great, he hasn't stop drinking since we got in the limo.

ANDREW. Everything will be fine, . You worry too much.

MAURIZIO. Ladies and Gentlemen, your organic gluten free watercress and goat cheese salads are being served.

(The song ends and everyone separates and moves off accordingly. MARIO stumbles over, already well on his way to getting drunk.)

MARIO. Anthony, I have to talk to you. Alone.

ANTHONY. Can it wait? There are tons of people I haven't even said hello to yet.

(ANTHONY and ANDREW walk off.)

MARIO. But Anthony –

(LUCIA approaches.)

LUCIA. Mario, what is going on with you tonight? You look like you just lost your best friend.

MARIO. Oh God, Lucia, this is awful.

LUCIA. Honey, I know you've never been a fan of Andrew's, but you have to get over it already.

MARIO. You don't understand. That's not it. Well, that is it, but I have a real reason now. Not that I didn't have a reason before, but –

(LUCIA pulls his drink away.)

LUCIA. Okay, you're done drinking. Thank you!

MARIO. Anthony's like a brother to me. I don't want to hurt him, but if I tell him then he'll be devastated. But if I don't, it will come out eventually anyway…oh, I just don't know what to do! What should I do?

LUCIA. Honey, I don't know what you're talking about, but the first thing you're going to do is get a nice espresso. No more of these, you're a mess.

(She puts her arm around him and they cross off.)

TONIANN. Angela, I knew I was gonna get *acida* from the eggplant.

ANGELA. There's nothing wrong with the eggplant.

(She waves to an audience member.)

TONIANN. Oh yeah? Did you see cousin Josphine? She went to the bathroom three times already. I counted.

ANGELA. Well, cousin Josephine's had diverticulitis for years, she should know what to eat by now.

(FRANKIE pulls "MRS. POLINSKI" off to the side.)

FRANKIE. Hey Rod-uh, Mrs. Polinski. So, listen…I know after this you and I are supposed to go on a date.

RODNEY. That's the deal.

FRANKIE. Can we just do coffee or something?

RODNEY. What, you don't want to get to know this?

FRANKIE. Not dressed like that!

RODNEY. I don't have to keep the Spanx on all night, baby. Have a few drinks, and then maybe I could convince you to come over to my place for a cocktail.

(**JOSEPH** *spots* "**MRS. POLINSKI**" *and comes over with a drink for her.*)

JOSEPH. Mrs. Polinski! Mrs. Polinsky!

"MRS. POLINSKI." Oh yes, that's me. Oh Gracias, I mean… *Grazie Prego*!

JOSEPH. Ahhh…you speak Italian, nice!

(*She raises her glass.*)

We'll make an Italian out of you yet!

"MRS POLINSKI." Well, my mother's family was Italian.

JOSEPH. Really? What part of Italy were they from?

"MRS POLINSKI." I'm gonna go ahead and say Sicily.

JOSEPH. I should've known. *Salute!*

"MRS POLINSKI." *Salaam aleikum* yourself.

(**MARIA** *comes over to* **JOSEPH.**)

MARIA. Daddy, what did you think of my song at the church?

JOSEPH. The best I ever heard, right, Mrs. Polinski? Can I call you by your first name?

"MRS. POLINSKI." Um…sure.

JOSEPH. What is it?

"MRS. POLINSKI." Oh, it's um….Zsa Zsa.

MARIA. Zsa Zsa! What a great name! Daddy maybe that could be my stage name, Zsa Zsa Pinnunziato!!

(**JOSEPH**'s *phone rings.* **TONIANN** *and* **ANGELA** *make their way over to hear* **JOSEPH.**)

Zsa Zsa, excuse me for one second I gotta take this.

(**RODNEY** *and* **MARIA** *cross away.*)

"MRS POLINSKI." You could be Lady Zsa Zsa.

JOSEPH. Yeah, Gary….get out of here, Lucky Lady hit! Naaah, I'm not busy. I'll come collect it now. Angela, I'll be right back.

ANGELA. Are you insane!? You can't leave your own son's wedding!

JOSEPH. Everyone's having a good time, everyone's tipped. Gary Gavone is at a bar two blocks away, I'll be back in a little bit.

*(**JOSEPH** leaves.)*

TONIANN. I can't believe he's running to go collect on a horse from Gary Gavone of all people.

ANGELA. I guess I should be happy it's just horses, and not some *conmare.* Speaking of *conmares* –

*(**TONIANN** takes a dramatic moment to collect herself.)*

TONIANN. Oh, Angela, I don't wanna talk about it.

ANGELA. Okay.

TONIANN. You're right, I should talk about it. So, I was at Bingo the other night, and just as I was about to get the four corners my cell phone rings,. I see it's Salvatore, so I answer. Only it's not Sal, it's his wife. And she tells me she's pregnant.

ANGELA. Oh my God! That two-timing bastard!

TONIANN. I was so devastated, that I left Bingo and went over to the café where he was playing cards, and I told him, "Salvatore Baccacalupe Giancarlo, you are dead to me." And then I went home and ate a pint of Häagen-Dazs.

*(**TONIANN** breaks down in tears, and **ANGELA** hugs her.)*

Why are all the good ones taken? Or gay?

*(**MAURIZIO** interupts, calling for everyone's attention.)*

MAURIZIO. All right everybody!

TONIANN. Or really gay?

MAURIZIO. Is everyone out there having a good time?

(They all clap and yell. The wedding guest heads up onstage, either alone or with two audience members.)

I said, is everyone having a good time?! Fabulous, just

what I love to hear. Now I think it's time for a little traditional and not so traditional dancing. Are we ready?

(They all clap and yell some more. The "Tarantella" comes on and everyone dances. The **WEDDING GUEST** *[ensemble] may bring some audience members to the stage to dance. "***MRS. POLINSKI***" is more and more intoxicated as the wedding goes on.)*

(The song ends and switches to a funky version of "The Chicken Dance." **MAURIZIO** *takes center stage.)*

MAURIZIO. Now we are going to do a little chicken dance, but this is the European chicken dance. Watch, I'll show you.

*(***MAURIZIO** *engages in a very original, gay version of the chicken dance, showing no humility what so ever. Everyone in the cast follows along, guiding the audience participants to play along. When the song is over, the guys usher the people back to their seats and the cast claps and celebrate throughout. The music now changes to another dance number and* **ANTHONY** *and* **ANDREW** *dance together, entwined and oblivious to what is going on around them.* **TONIANN** *breaks out into her own dance solo while* **MARIO, FRANKIE, CONNIE** *and* **LUCIA** *break out into another dance number, including audience members where possible.)*

*("***MRS. POLINSKI***" who is now at this point completely inebriated, takes a very intoxicated* **FRANKIE** *onto the dance floor as they dance like animals in heat. It gets dangerously close to them being spotted but they manage to stay under the radar until* **AUNT TONIANN** *starts to watch them and is immediately confused.* **LUCIA** *in fear that* **ANGELA** *may notice grabs her and turns her away from the scene. Every time* **ANGELA** *starts to turn in the direction of the dancers,* **LUCIA** *grabs her attention back.)*

LUCIA. Mrs. Pinnunziato, I just wanted to tell you what a lovely job you did tonight.

ANGELA. Thank you, Lucia. But I have to give Maurizio LeGrande the credit on this one.

LUCIA. But the food! The food was just incredible.

ANGELA. Lucia, please tell me, what did you think of the eggplant? Too spicy?

*(While **LUCIA** is distracting **ANGELA**, **ANTHONY** and **ANDREW** come over and separate **FRANKIE** and "**MRS. POLINSKI.**" **ANTHONY** now dances with **FRANKIE** while **ANDREW** dances with his "mother.")*

LUCIA. Not too spicy at all, Angela.

ANGELA. Thank you so much for saying that Lucia, my sister gets me so paranoid. Oh look!

*(**LUCIA** cringes, afraid of what **ANGELA** is seeing.)*

Andrew is dancing with his mother! So beautiful. I'm so glad she came up from Florida for the wedding.

*(**FATHER ROSALIA** enters, **ANGELA** sees him and rushes over. **ANTHONY** sees this and immediately goes into panic mode.)*

ANGELA. Father Rosalia?

ANTHONY. Ahhhhhhhhhhhhhhhhhh!

ANGELA. Ahhhhhhhhhhhhhhhhhh!

ANTHONY. Ahhhhhhhhhhhhhhhh!

ANGELA. Ahhh?????????

ANTHONY. Mom, cousin Josephine is having a panic attack outside.

ANGELA. I have Xanax in my bag! Excuse me, Father. I'm coming Josephine! I'm coming!

*(**ANGELA** pulls a pill bottle from her purse and rushes off.)*

ANTHONY. Father Rosalia, what brings you here?

FATHER ROSALIA. Well Anthony, I felt so bad that I was unable to perform the service that I wanted to come in person to at least give my blessing.

ANTHONY. Father that was so not necessary, so, so not necessary.

(tries to usher him out)

Well, Father, I know you must be so busy, thank you so much for dropping by –

FATHER ROSALIA. Not at all, actually I noticed some of the food when I walked in, it looks absolutely incredible.

ANTHONY. It's horrible don't eat it. My poor Aunt is getting so sick, she can barely move!

*(He tries again to get him to go, but **AUNT TONIANN** comes running over. **ANDREW** immediately follows. **TONIANN** flanks the **PRIEST**, rubbing his arm.)*

TONIANN. Ohh! Father Rosalia! How do you feel?

FATHER ROSALIA. Wonderful. God has given these two men such a beautiful day for their wedding.

ANTHONY. Yes, yes. He has given us such a beautiful day. And isn't it a shame that we have to be inside on such a beautiful day, but you don't Father, so thank you for coming –

TONIANN. Oh Anthony, don't rush the man, he might be hungry.

FATHER ROSALIA. Everything does look so delicious.

TONIANN. Oh, it is!

ANTHONY. Aunt Toniann, tell him how spicy and horrible the food is.

TONIANN. Come with me, Father, I'll keep you away from that nasty eggplant. But the lobster oreganata is to die for!

FATHER ROSALIA. There's lobster?

(She takes him off.)

ANDREW. What is he doing here?

ANTHONY. He felt bad and now he wants to give his blessing.

ANDREW. And now we have to make him leave.

ANTHONY. I know! Go stick an ex-lax in his lobster!

(**ANGELA** *comes back in.*)

ANGELA. Anthony everything was fine with cousin Josephine. What made you think she was having a panic attack?

ANTHONY. She's not?

ANGELA. No, but she took the drugs anyway...

ANDREW. Mrs. Pinnunziato...did you say hello to my friend Judith?

ANGELA. No! I'm sorry Andrew...did you want me to meet her?

ANDREW. I actually told her about your pasta fagioli and she's dying for the recipe.

ANGELA. Oh God, it's so easy! I'll go give it to her. Anything for my new son-in-law! Judith, honey, get a pen.

(*She pinches his cheeks and goes. A tipsy* **MARIO** *comes over to* **ANTHONY**.)

MARIO. Anthony, I have to talk to you now.

ANTHONY. Mario, I have big drama going on, can it wait?

MARIO. No. Yes. I don't know!

ANDREW. Ok, why don't you give me the drink, and we'll get you some coffee.

MARIO. Don't touch me! I know what you did and I hate you, Andrew. I hate you and everything about you!

(**MARIO** *tries to pull his drink back and instead it gets all over* **ANDREW**.)

ANTHONY. Mario!

MARIO. I'm sorry, Anthony. But I can't take it anymore. I just can't hold it in.

ANDREW. Mario, calm down and you and me can go somewhere and talk, just the two of us.

MARIO. I'm not going anywhere with you, you lying bastard!

ANDREW. Mario please stop...

MARIO. Anthony, I have to talk to you. Please. Can't we just leave now? Just us?

ANTHONY. Mario, sweetie, anything you have to say you can say in front of my new husband.

MARIO. Oh God, he's your husband…

(**MARIO** *now starts to have a real panic attack.* **GREGO-RIO** *crosses over to* **MARIO**.)

CONNIE. Oh jeez, Mario is like two sheeps to the wind.

MARIA. *(and others nearby)* Sheets.

GREGORIO. Is Mario okay? He seems upset.

MARIO. This is all his fault!

ANDREW. Mario, please calm down. Not now.

MARIO. Anthony you shouldn't have to go through this.

ANTHONY. Go through what?

(**GREGORIO** *jumps in before* **MARIO** *can answer.*)

GREGORIO. Mario is right. Anthony, there is something you need to know. Everyone!

(**GREGORIO** *clings his glass with a spoon. Everyone reacts and starts to draw near.*)

MARIA. What's going on?

TONIANN. Oh, it's the toast.

(**GREGORIO** *speaks over the crowd.*)

GREGORIO. Everyone can I have your attention please.

ANDREW. Don't do this.

GREGORIO. Someday you'll thank me. Everyone, it's time you all learned the truth about Andrew. You see last year –

MARIO. You jealous bitch!!!

(**MARIO** *gets out of the chair and lunges for* **GREGO-RIO**. *The two start to cat fight and everyone breaks them apart. In breaking them apart,* **CONNIE** *pushes* **LUCIA** *out of the way.*)

LUCIA. Don't push me!

CONNIE. Can't you see there is a problem here!

LUCIA. I was trying to break them up.

CONNIE. And as usual you're getting in the way…

LUCIA. I've had it with you, Connie…

CONNIE. Why can't you mind your business…

RODNEY. Girls, girls, lez-be-friends!

(LUCIA and CONNIE now break into a fight, pulling each other's hair and screaming mild profanity ad libs. FRANKIE and "MRS. POLINSKI" come to the rescue and break them apart. In doing so, CONNIE goes to grab LUCIA's hair and pulls off "MRS. POLINSKI's" wig instead. Everyone stands around horror stricken, including ANGELA, AUNT TONIANN, and FATHER ROSALIA who have progressively made it back onstage during the fights.)

TONIANN. Oh my God…it's a Puerto Rican?

ALL. Venezuelan.

ANGELA. Whatever! I want to know what's going on and I want to know now!

ANTHONY. Ma, I can explain.

ANGELA. I think you better start.

ANDREW. It was my fault, Mrs. Pinnunziato. Anthony didn't know this wasn't really my mother.

FATHER ROSALIA. This is a man?!

(FATHER ROSALIA 'peeks' at RODNEY's chest, and RODNEY slaps his hand away.)

RODNEY. Excuse you!

ANGELA. I appreciate you trying to cover up for my son Andrew but I have no doubt in my mind that Anthony knew quite well about all this.

ANTHONY. Oh God, this wasn't supposed to happen.

ANGELA. You're damn right this wasn't supposed to happen! Do you take me and your father for fools!? I can't believe you would embarrass me like this. I asked was for two very simple things. The blessing of Andrew's real mother, and for Father Rosalia to perform the service, which I obviously overlooked due to the poor man's kidney stones.

FATHER ROSALIA. Kidney stones?

ANDREW. Oh God.

MARIA. Oh Jesus!

CONNIE. Oh shit!

FATHER ROSALIA. Who said I had kidney stones?

(ANGELA *takes a moment to absorb this and crosses down stage completely mortified.*)

ANGELA. Please tell me Father that you were suffering from kidney stones.

FATHER ROSALIA. No, thank God!

ANGELA. I'm gonna faint! I'm gonna pass out. Maria, Toniann, get me a chair!

(*They do so and she sits, popping a handful of Xanax.*)

MAURIZIO. Everyone please there is no reason for the freaking out. We have a fabulous Venetian hour coming out any –

(ANGELA *jumps up and yells.*)

ANGELA. Fuck the Venetian hour!! This wedding is over! Everyone go home!

ANTHONY. Mom, you're completely overreacting to all this. If you would just calm down and listen to reason....

ANGELA. Listen to reason? Listen to reason?!? Is this how I raised you!? You sabotage your whole wedding and of all things you could possibly do Anthony, you go and lie to a Goddamn priest!

(*Everyone gasps.*)

Excuse me, Father, but I'm really losing it.

FATHER ROSALIA. Yes. Well. I have to get going. I have a, um, a Bat Mitzvah to get to.

(**FATHER ROSALIA** *does the sign of the cross, then leaves.*)

TONIANN. Angela, take a deep breath and let's discuss this.

ANGELA. Anthony, what you did today was the worst thing you could ever do to me. I am so hurt right now I can't even breathe. God will punish you for this, Anthony... you hear me, GOD WILL PUNISH YOU!

GREGORIO. But since he's not here…allow me.

(Everyone is completely stunned as **GREGORIO** *steps forward.)*

As I was saying, before I got so rudely interrupted. Anthony, there is something you need to hear about your new husband.

ANTHONY. What?

GREGORIO. While you were off having a Memorial Day barbeque with all the lesbians, Andrew was with me in Fire Island. And I mean *with* me. Your whole wedding to him is a joke. He can stand up and take any vow he wants, but the party will always start and end with Andrew Polinski. And trust me, Anthony, in time you will be nothing but an afterthought, a "mistake" that Andrew will pretend never happened.

(He crosses over to **ANDREW***.)*

GREGORIO. *(cont.)* Good thing this wedding wasn't legal. Just think of how much you'll save on the divorce.

*(***GREGORIO*** exits, crossing with* **JOSEPH***, who is returning from collecting on his bet and is oblivious.)*

AUNT TONIANN. Wow, and yous call me a bitch?

JOSEPH. Did I miss the cake?

(No one answers.)

What? What'd I miss?

ANTHONY. Andrew, please tell me that's not true.

*(***ANDREW*** is speechless.)*

Is that true?

ANDREW. Only technically!

RODNEY. And I was your mother!!

*(***RODNEY*** walks away sobbing.* **ANDREW** *makes an effort to plead his case.)*

ANDREW. Anthony, please you have to understand that when we met…I was so scared and unsure because I had feelings for you that I never had with anyone else. I guess a part of me panicked. I was in Fire Island and trying to really see if I even wanted to be in a relationship. I got tanked, and yes…I had a fling with Gregorio. But –

JOSEPH. Hold on a second, Tiger Woods. You cheated, on my son, and then you went and made your *conmare*, your best man at my son's wedding?!

(**JOSEPH** *reaches into his coat pocket. Everyone gasps and ducks.*)

RODNEY. He's got a gun!

(**JOSEPH** *pulls out a handkerchief, mops his forehead, then throws it to the ground.*)

Oh, it's just a handkerchief.

JOSEPH. I'll kill you, you bastard!

(**JOSEPH** *lunges for* **ANDREW**, *but misses.* **ANTHONY** *starts to hyperventilate.*)

ANTHONY. Dad, stop! How could you do this to me? Oh God, I'm gonna faint. I'm gonna pass out! Maria, Toniann, get me a chair!

MAURIZIO. Oh my God, it's genetic.

ANDREW. It meant nothing. No, actually, that's not true. It meant everything because it made me realize just how incredible what we had was. I remember one morning, when we were cuddled up in bed, I got this feeling – I just didn't want to let go. I never felt that way before. I love you. I want to be with you. I know I should have told you, I was just so afraid of losing you. I can't lose you.

(**ANTHONY** *is silent, too devastated to respond. His mother steps up.*)

ANTHONY. Andrew, I –

ANGELA. Andrew, you are a liar and a cheat…You are not welcome in this family. Stay the hell away from my son and get out!

(**ANDREW** *starts to go.* **ANTHONY** *starts to speak, but his mother shushes him.* **ANDREW** *turns back, but* **ANTHONY** *says nothing more, so he goes.* **ANGELA** *goes to* **ANTHONY** *and hugs him as they reconcile in tears. Everyone is consoling anthony when a* **WEDDING GUEST** *[ensemble] comes over hysterically sobbing.*)

WEDDING GUEST. Oh my God, Anthony! I can't believe this. I am so sorry sweety. I know exactly how you feel. Listen, if you need anything, anything at all, do not hesitate to call me. I will be sleeping by the phone!

(**ANTHONY** *nods.*)

I love you!

(*The* **GUEST** *kisses him and leaves.*)

ANTHONY. I love you, too. (*There is an awkward moment of silence.*) Mom?

ANGELA. What baby?

ANDREW. Who was that?

ANGELA. I have no freakin idea.

(*Everyone looks confused.* **MAURIZIO** *dashes over.*)

MAURIZIO. That was Vera Marinelli, of the Bensonhurst and Todt Hill Marinielli's. And how do I know this, I hear you asking in your pea-sized little brains. I'll tell you how. I've been running around like a crazy person collecting envelopes of money from all your crazy family for YOU to go on a honeymoon with HIM, and HIM just left the building!!! So he tickled another boy's pickle? So what? Make it work people! My reputation is at stake!

(**MARIO**, **LUCIA** *and* **CONNIE** *come over to* **ANTHONY**.)

MARIO. I tried to tell you, Anthony.

LUCIA. You knew? You knew and you didn't say anything?

MARIO. I found out yesterday. He wouldn't talk to me! I didn't want him to hear it like this, in front of everyone!

ANTHONY. I loved him, and despite what he did, I still do.

RODNEY. Of course you do, baby. He's got an ass like a Kardashian.

ANTHONY. We were supposed to go to Paris for our honeymoon.

MAURIZIO. Well, you know what they say in Paris, one minute everything is oui oui, the next minute poo poo.

(**MAURIZIO** *exits.* **MARIA** *and* **AUNT TONIANN** *go to* **ANGELA.**)

TONIANN. Not for nothing, *Papa* always said, never trust the Polish.

ANGELA. As far as I'm concerned there is nothing that boy could do to make up for what he did to my son.

TONIANN. If he was Italian –

(*Suddenly music is heard, and* **ANDREW** *reappears and serenades* **ANTHONY** *with a romantic version of "My Italian Boy." Everyone watches in complete amazement as* **ANDREW** *sings from his heart to win* **ANTHONY** *over.*[*])

ANDREW.

I'M GONNA LOVE YOU BABY

I'M GONNA LOVE MY ITALIAN BOY

YOUR LOVE FULFILLS ME THROUGH THE CHILLS AND KEEPS ME WARM

YOU'RE A SENSATION

IT'S LIKE A VACATION WHEN YOU'RE NEAR

I SEE US TOGETHER THROUGH ANY WEATHER RAIN OR STORM

(**MAURIZIO** *suddenly pops up and hands him a microphone.*)

YOUR SMILE IS GOLDEN

AND 'TIL I'M OLD AND GREY I KNOW

I'M GONNA COVER YOU WITH LOVE FROM HEAD TO TOE

YOU'RE GONNA FEEL IT WHEREVER YOU GO

I'M GONNA LOVE YOU BABY, I'M GONNA LOVE MY ITALIAN BOY

---

[*] Please see "A Note About the Music" on Page 4.

'CAUSE IT'S BELLISSIMO WHEN I'M KISSIN' MI AMORE!
I'M GONNA LOVE YOU SUGAR, I'M GONNA LOVE MY
ITALIAN BOY
I SAY "MOLTO BELLO!" TO MY FELLOW I ADORE

TI AMO!
Forgive me!
MY ITALIAN BOY!

(**ANTHONY** *is swept off his feet and when* **ANDREW** *has completed the song he hugs him as everyone around claps for them.*)

ANTHONY. Andrew, you sang! In front of everyone!

ANDREW. Don't you know I would do anything for you?

ANTHONY. And it was very good!

ANDREW. Don't throw us away, Anthony. Let's prove them all wrong. We can do this. Stay married to me.

(**ANTHONY** *looks to everyone for their opinion, the family nods in approval. He looks to the audience, who will of course approve.*)

ANTHONY. I'll stay married to you!

(*They embrace.* **MAURIZIO** *re-enters, carrying a suitcase.*)

MAURIZIO. Thank God, I stopped everyone from going home. See everyone, just a little snag and everything is fine now. As I always say, to forget is human, but to sing a very random love song at the last minute in order to save your marriage is divine. So boys, I've been counting the envelopes and it looks like you will have lots of money to spend in gay Paris.

ANTHONY. Let's go, baby!

(**ANTHONY** *tosses the bouquet behind him.* **LUCIA** *and* **CONNIE** *jointly catch the bouquet and look at each other with love in their eyes, then kiss as a few chords of the wedding march play.*)

MAURIZIO. I do the Lesbian Weddings, too!

(*curtain call*)

ADDENDUM A:

If "Rodney" is portrayed by an African-American actor, the following changes can be made:

ACT I, SCENE IV: REGINA PACIS CHURCH
replaces page 37

LUCIA. I'm saying that I think we both know someone who could fit the role. And well.

ANDREW. We do?

LUCIA. Come on, who's the girliest mother hen you know?

ANDREW. Uh, well, Rodney, but –

LUCIA. Exactly!

ANDREW. But Rodney is Black!

LUCIA. So?

ANDREW. Whatever! My mother's Polish!

LUCIA. Well, there are black people in Poland. Aren't there?

ANDREW. You think?

LUCIA. Definitely. Well, we'll just say she lives by a beach. Trust me, no one will notice.

ANDREW. Do you really think that will work?

LUCIA. It will have to.

ANDREW. Ok, then what about the priest?

LUCIA. That part's easy. I'm sure we can find a minister online.

ANDREW. But his mother wants Father Rosalia.

LUCIA. Don't worry, I have a plan.

ACT I, SCENE V: BACCI'S
replaces pg 41

LUCIA. What do you think of Rodney?

FRANKIE. Isn't he supposed to be here?

ANDREW. He's not going to be in the bridal party any more.

LUCIA. He's going to be dressing up as Andrew's mother.

FRANKIE. Whoa! That's serious shit!

ANDREW. We made a deal with him so Anthony's mother won't pull the plug on the whole wedding.

FRANKIE. A deal? But, how's that gonna work, he's **black.**

LUCIA. And there are black people in Poland.

FRANKIE. Whatever. Look, I've seen this on Jerry Springer… it ain't gonna work.

ANDREW. We have to make it work. There's no other option.

FRANKIE. Okay. But what does any of this have to do with me?

LUCIA. That's where the whole 'deal' part comes in.

ANDREW. He said he would do it in exchange for a date with you.

FRANKIE. ME?! Why me?

ACT II, RECEPTION
replaces pg 62

"MRS POLINSKY." Oh! Da! Da!

(They start to dance. AUNT TONIANN is now using hairspray on the stain. ANTHONY decides it's good enough and goes back to the dance floor with ANDREW.)

ANTHONY. Are you nuts? I can't believe you dressed up Rodney as your mother! **I told my whole family you were Polish!**

ANDREW. **Lucia says there are black people in Poland.**

(ANTHONY looks at him stunned.)

ANTHONY. **Wow! You really are Polish.**

ANDREW. Whatever. It's working perfectly. Look at him, he's doing great.

ANTHONY. Oh yeah great, he hasn't stopped drinking since we got in the limo.

ANDREW. Everything will be fine. You worry too much.

MAURIZIO. Ladies and Gentlemen, your organic gluten free watercress and goat cheese salads are being served.

(The song ends and everyone separates and moves off accordingly. MARIO stumbles over, already well on his way to getting drunk.)

MARIO. Anthony, I have to talk to you. Alone.

ANTHONY. Can it wait? There are tons of people I haven't even said hello to yet.

(ANTHONY and ANDREW walk off.)

TONIANN. Oh yeah? Did you see cousin Josphine? She went to the bathroom three times already. I counted.

ANGELA. Well, cousin Josephine's had diverticulitis for years, she should know what to eat by now.

*(**FRANKIE** pulls "**MRS. POLINSKI**" off to the side.)*

FRANKIE. Hey Rod-uh, Mrs. Polinski. So, listen…I know after this you and I are supposed to go on a date.

RODNEY. That's the deal.

FRANKIE. Can we just do coffee or something?

RODNEY. What, you don't want to get to know this?

FRANKIE. Not dressed like that!

RODNEY. I don't have to keep the spanx on all night baby. Have a few drinks, and then maybe I could convince you to come over to my place for a cocktail. **'Cause know what they say: "You never go back, once you go Polish."**

*(**JOSEPH** spots "**MRS. POLINSKI**" and comes over with a drink for her.)*

JOSEPH. Mrs. Polinski! Mrs. Polinsky!

"MRS. POLINSKI." Oh yes, that's me. Oh Gracias, I mean… *Grazie Prego*!

JOSEPH. Ahhh…you speak Italian, nice.

ACT II, RECEPTION
replaces page 71

(**MARIO** *gets out of the chair and lunges for* **GREGO-RIO**. *The two start to cat fight and everyone breaks them apart. In breaking them apart,* **CONNIE** *pushes* **LUCIA** *out of the way.*)

LUCIA. Don't push me!

CONNIE. Can't you see there is a problem here!

LUCIA. I was trying to break them up.

CONNIE. And as usual you're getting in the way...

LUCIA. I've had it with you, Connie...

CONNIE. Why can't you mind your business...

RODNEY. Girls, girls, lez-be-friends!

(**LUCIA** *and* **CONNIE** *now break into a fight, pulling each other's hair and screaming mild profanity ad libs.* **FRANKIE** *and* "**MRS. POLINSKI**" *come to the rescue and break them apart. In doing so,* **CONNIE** *goes to grab* **LUCIA**'s *hair and pulls off* "**MRS. POLINSKI**'s" *wig instead. Everyone stands around horror stricken, including* **ANGELA**, **AUNT TONIANN** *and* **FATHER ROSALIA** *who have progressively made it back on stage during the fights.*)

TONIANN. Oh my God...She's black!

ANGELA. Whatever! I want to know what's going on and I want to know now!

ANTHONY. Ma, I can explain.

OTHER TITLES AVAILABLE FROM SAMUEL FRENCH

THE AWESOME 80'S PROM

Ken Davenport & The Class of '89

Comedy, Audience Participation, Interactive / 11m, 8f / Unit Set

The Awesome 80s Prom is a brand new blast-from-the-past party in the style of *Tony 'n Tina's Wedding* and *The Donkey Show* set at Wanaget High's Senior Prom... in 1989! All your favorite characters from your favorite '80s movies are at THE PROM, from the Captain of the Football Team to the Asian Exchange Student, from the Geek to the hottie Head Cheerleader, and they're all competing for Prom King and Queen. And just like on "American Idol", the audience decides who wins! Come back in time and join the breakdance circle or just sit back and watch the '80s drama unfold.

WINNER! 2006 IMPROV THEATER AWARD - "BEST INTERACTIVE SHOW"

OTHER TITLES AVAILABLE FROM SAMUEL FRENCH

THE ALTOS

David Landau
Music and Lyrics by Nikki Stern

Like *The Sopranos*, only lower!

Musical Comedy / 4m, 3f / Interior

An Interactive Musical Comedy Mystery Spoof of the famous HBO series. Meet the family that inspired it all, the Altos. It's Tony's funeral (Or is it?) and his wife Toffee has invited you to the wake. Chris wants you should check your weapons at the door (and if you don't have any, he's got extras!) Uncle Senior has a rigged dice game going and Tony's Ma is - well just nuts. Tony's shrink Dr. Malaise is giving free analysis and the Father isn't sure what he is doing! But one thing is for sure, almost no one seems sad that Tony is gone and they certainly don't seem happy once he's discovered alive. Be prepared to dodge bullets, laugh at the songs and see if you can't figure out who put a contract out on Tony!

OTHER TITLES AVAILABLE FROM SAMUEL FRENCH

ALL ABOARD THE MARRIAGE HEARSE

Matt Morillo

Dramatic Comedy / 1m, 1f / Simple Set

Sean and Amy are your typical co-habitating, Catholic/Jewish, twenty-something couple living in Manhattan. They work hard, love each other and share common goals in life. Well, sort of. After nearly three years together, Amy wants to get married but Sean does not believe in the institution. The game is on!!! Tonight is the night when they will settle the marriage question once and for all. They will both bring their "A" game and the gloves will come off. Sean will try to talk her out of it. Amy will try to talk him into it. Will they break up? Will they keep going on the path they're on? Will they climb aboard the "Marriage Hearse?" It's the perfect show for anyone who has ever been married, will be married, wants to be married, doesn't want to be married, has thought about getting married, has been told they should be married, knows someone who is married, knows someone who wants to be married, knows someone who was married, knows someone who should be married, knows someone who shouldn't be married, has parents who are married, has parents who were married, has parents who shouldn't be married, and everyone else! What else would you expect from the team that brought you *Angry Young Women In Low-Rise Jeans With High-Class Issues?*

OTHER TITLES AVAILABLE FROM SAMUEL FRENCH

DEVIL BOYS FROM BEYOND

Buddy Thomas and Kenneth Elliott
Based on an original script by Buddy Thomas
Original Song, *Sensitive Girl*, music and lyrics by
Drew Fornarola

Comedy / 4m, 4f (all female roles can be played by men in drag) / Unit Set

Flying Saucers! Backstabbing Bitches! Muscle Hunks and Men in Pumps! Wake up and smell the alien invasion in this outrageous comedy by Kenneth Elliott and Buddy Thoman, the author of the Off Broadway hit play, *Crumple Zone*.

"Drag heaven on Earth...DEVIL BOYS is a riot."
– *The New York Times*

"What's funnier than a Pulitzer Prize-winning journalist investigating reports of flying saucers in the mysterious swamplands of Lizard Lick, Florida—the hickest hick-town in all of America? Not much! Unless, perhaps, you cast a man in drag, add a boozing ex-husband, a nemesis/rival reporter, to boot! Mix in clever one-liners, a candy-colored design, and enough boy-toy eye-candy to fill a giant's Halloween sack, and you've got one hell of a show! You might want see it twice. I missed some lines, here and there, as I was still belly-laughing from some previous ones."
– *NYTheatre.com*

"A gaily goofy all-male sci-fi adventure. Nuttier than a pack of killer tomatoes."
–*CitysBest.com*

"Hilarious. This play will roughly triple the Theatre District's laugh quotient for as long as it's able to camp out."
–*TalkinBroadway.com*

SAMUELFRENCH.COM

MAR 31 2011

LaVergne, TN USA
27 February 2011
218146LV00006B/23/P